The Royal Dorgis

Bernadette Crepeau

Wishing you the Very best! Love Bernadette

Bernadette Crepeau

This book is dedicated to my brilliant editor and dear friend,
Lynne Borden

The great men & women serving in
The Armed Forces

The wonderful folks at
The Royal British Legion
Battersea, England

And in loving memory of
Polly, Mick, & John Regan
& Peter Kerins

Acknowledgment

With each book, I meet the most incredibly generous people who willingly give their time and talent to help me tell my stories. This book is no exception. Any mistakes are mine alone.

Note from Bernadette

On a trip to Ireland, I was inspired by the beauty and legends of this ancient land to tell the story of the Brooklyn Leprechaun. I quickly wrote a trilogy that included: The Brooklyn Leprechaun, Royal Spirits, and Magical Scotland.

Then I was inspired to write a screenplay by the same name. In doing so, I realized my trilogy included too much of a back-story and not enough action. For those of you that have read the first trilogy, I hope you enjoy the differences. For those of you that are new to the magical world of **Bridget** and the **Royal Dorgis,** please enjoy.

With Love,

Bernadette

Cast of Characters
& Places

Bridget
Born in Brooklyn, N.Y. She inherited land in Ireland and the gift of Magic. Erie is where she also meets her immortal ancestors and the fae folk.

Battersea British Legion
Actual place and wonderful people. Names and descriptions of people are my imagination at work.

Cathcart
Holding place for fae under Morrigan's influence.

Dorgis
In 2007, Queen Elizabeth II had four **Dorgis** (dachshund-Corgi **crossbreeds**): Cider, Berry, Vulcan, and Candy.

Friar Xavier
Friar Francis Xavier is a five-hundred-year-old spirit in service to the royal family.

Geraldine,
Faeire, Queen of all fae, and Bridget's many time's removed great-grandmother.

Michelle
Born and raised in France. She is the veterinary assistant to the Queen's prized dogs.

Mick aka Lord Howth
A handsome wizard, Bridget first met in the guise of a Brittany spaniel when he mentored her in all things magic.

Morrigan
Geraldine's cousin and Goddess of War who Bridget defeated in battle.

Peter Kerins

Bridget's cousin, a private detective who lives in England.

Padraig

Is King of the Leprechauns, husband to Queen Geraldine and Bridget's loveable many times removed great-grandfather.

Que-tip

An English, feisty teen faeire with cotton ball hair.

Stan

Military slang for Afghanistan.

Chapter 1

Barnacogue Palace
Bridget's Bedroom
County Mayo, Ireland

"Crack on mate! Get a bloody move on! Shut those yappers up; we don't have all day!"

"Shut it; they'll be quiet as the grave soon enough."

Bridget's heart beats fast and loud, her palms sweat. She can hear the men arguing, all the more frightening for the anger and evil in their quiet whispers. She knows something horrific is happening and runs to see what the problem is.

A small golden-haired puppy, no bigger than a child's football, is picked up by a large gloved hand. The puppy slips free only to be roughly captured again. He yelps in pain, then silence. Others are crying in fear, some bark in anger. She keeps running, getting no closer. She feels the slippery stones beneath her feet. Her chest tightens. She is cold with fear. Hot tears run down her face, one by one the puppies are silenced. NO! She cries out. They don't stop. The puppies are silent.

Bridget shivers uncontrollably; buries her head in her wet pillow. "It's a dream...thank God it's only a dream!" She sits up lightheaded and staggers to the bathroom. "Wow, that was a bad one."

Bridget often remembers parts of her nightmares. Usually, she is pursued by some unknown evil. This is new. She never wakes up crying and sick to her stomach. She turns the faucet on and soaks a washcloth in near-scalding water and holds it to her face. The throbbing in her head eases, but the fear in her heart remains. Bridget can't stop shivering. *All I remember is that I'm too late to save them. But who do I need to save and where are they?*

Bridget enters the palace dining room not sure she feels well enough to eat anything.

"Well good morning Bridget, now don't you look like something the cat dragged in," Mick says jokingly, although he is very concerned about how pale and shaken his friend looks.

Bridget helps herself to a glass of fresh orange juice from the sideboard that has every type of breakfast food anyone could ever want. She pulls out an ornate, red velvet chair and sits across from Mick.

When she first met Lord Michael Howth, he appeared to her as a dog, and she called him Mick. She loved that she could talk to him about anything. But now, that she knows he's human, she finds herself hesitating to talk with him about anything she's feeling, for fear of sounding silly. Not only is Mick a wizard who still looks twenty-one, even though he was born in the eighteen hundreds, but he is also absolutely gorgeous.

Mick waits patiently, watching Bridget as she stares at her crystal goblet. He pushes his half-eaten plate away and puts his elbows on the table, "Okay, out with it. What's troubling you?"

"A bad dream."

"Want to talk about it?" Mick asks quietly.

"It just left me feeling upset; I'll live. I do have something to tell you. The last time I was in London with Fergus, I had a feeling of impending doom. Something was wrong, not then, it was a feeling that something was going to be very wrong. Like a foreshadowing of what was to come. Sounds crazy huh?"

Bridget takes a sip of her juice dreading what she has to say next. Still looking at her glass, she says, "I thought it was weird and shook the feeling off. Now that I'm more familiar with my magical gifts, I trust my feelings. I need to go to London. I spoke with Fergus earlier to see if he wanted to come along, but he has some Dryad thing to take care of. But he does want me to meet a friend of his after I've seen the sights, a Friar Xavier. I guess he has a problem that may need a mortal to solve. The Friar is a spirit, but any friend of Fergus will be good company."

"You should not go alone. We may have stopped Morrigan, but there are still some of her foul creatures out there that want revenge."

"I know, but everyone's busy cleaning up after the Fae War. It has been six months, and there's still plenty of work to do." Bridget looks down at her plate, not wanting to look at her best friend. Biting her lip to stop from crying, she says, "I can't ask anyone to babysit me. Besides, I could use some alone time."

Mick is stunned at this news. Bridget is always smiling and filling the palace with her laughter. Everyone loves the young American. His castle in Scotland feels empty when she is not in it. Bridget worked hard to make sure that the castle woods were restored to their original condition, and all the animals were safe before she came home to Ireland to help restore the damaged homes and land at Barnacogue.

Perhaps she has been working too hard. He looks down at her pale blonde head bent over her glass and decided to let her go on her own. "You must promise to be in touch daily. Otherwise, I will be at your side and have you surrounded by warriors."

After a moment, Bridget looks at him. Her sea green eyes are smiling at the concern in his voice, "I promise to stay in touch. Hey, don't worry, I'm a New Yorker, London will be a walk in the park. "

Chapter 2

**St. James Park
London, England**

Bridget takes a seat on one of the many stone benches placed at various spots around the park. She still feels the dregs of the nightmare. It's hanging on like a bad slasher movie, the kind that makes you feel weird for days. She hopes the fresh air will help her feel better.

It helps that the sky would sometimes part its gray clouds to show a peek of clear sky. It's a little damp but not too cold. It's a blowing, slightly wet spring day in England. But an okay day to be outside.

There is something unique about the Irish and Londoners and their relationship with rain. If they had this rain in Brooklyn people would be rushing around wanting to get indoors. Here, people call it a soft mist and act as though it's a sunny spring day.

Bridget loves to watch people. She always thought to have the time to sit and do nothing except watch people would be fun. It's not. It's boring. She watches three guys about to walk past her bench. Two of the men dressed in dark business suits covered by beige raincoats are strolling like they're not getting wet, and Bridget is holding an umbrella and wearing a raincoat. She feels kind of silly, but heck, the mist is wet. She looks at the third man following close behind the first two.

The third man looks really dry. Bridget wonders if it's the large, brimmed hat he is wearing. Maybe she should get one. Even the hat looks dry, what gives with that? She looks closer and sees that he is carrying a walking stick, and by the look on his face, he would like to use it on the other two. The two men in front are busy talking and don't seem to be paying him any attention. Bridget wonders if they are ignoring him and that's what got his blood boiling?

The closer the third man gets the more he looks like the crime-solving monk on the BBC show her aunt Polly loves to watch. His gray wool habit looks ancient and ragged, clear evidence of his vow of poverty. Around his waist is a rope with three knots tied in it. A large, old, wooden rosary and cross hang from the rope. He's wearing leather sandals. With these puddles, his feet must be soaked. She didn't think they wore habits like that anymore. She wonders if he has one of those monk-like hairstyles that look like fringe surrounding a bald spot.

The third man, or monk guy, stops and stares at Bridget. She feels a whispery chill and shivers. She hopes he didn't catch her staring at him and got offended? She looks away, stares at a tree and pretends to be absorbed in watching the light mist add a sparkle to the leaves. *Yikes, he's coming over.*

"Pardon me Miss. Can you see me?"

"Well yes, I'm sorry; I didn't mean to stare. I'm a tourist," Bridget stammers from embarrassment.

"You can see and hear me?" He has a stunned look on his round, friendly face.

"Of course, shouldn't I?"

"No one has for a very, very long time. Please let me introduce myself; I am Friar Francis Xavier from Hamptons Court Monastery."

"Oh, you are Friar Xavier!"

The Friar bows his head, "To whom do I have the pleasure of speaking?"

"Oh, I'm sorry, my name is Bridget. I'm from Brooklyn, New York, pleased to meet you."

He looks at the beautiful young girl before him. Her long, pale blonde hair, breathtaking green eyes, and a generous smile fit the description. Bridget is so young; he can't believe his eyes, the young woman who defeated Morrigan and saved the entire Fae race, is a teenager? To confirm her identity, he asks, "Do you happen to know my friend, Fergus?"

Bridget laughs when she looks into the ageless face and sad light blue eyes. *Of course, I would just happen to meet Fergus' friend No wonder I was led to sit on a bench in the rain.* She looks at her ghostly companion and wonders why he looks uncomfortable. "I'm happy to meet you, I guess it should scare me a little that you're a spirit, but it doesn't really. You see I'm Irish, and after meeting some folks in Ireland recently, nothing surprises me. Fergus mentioned you, and I was going to contact you as soon as I settled in."

"Right then, may I visit with you a moment?" The friar asks as he hovers above the bench seat.

"Of course, I'd love the company."

Friar Xavier notices a hint of sadness in her voice and gently asks, "Are you missing your family?"

"That's part of it, without Mick, I feel lost."

"Is Mick your special fellow?"

Bridget laughs. "Mick is special all right. Since you're a spirit, then you'll understand. Mick, the dog, was a gift from my ancestors. He's a wizard named Lord Michael Howth. For a long time, I thought he was a special talking dog. He looked like an ordinary Brittany spaniel. It turns out that he is a human wizard and was sent to be my teacher or mentor into the world of the fae folk. We were seldom apart, and I miss him."

"Did you say a talking dog?"

"Well, he didn't speak out loud, he spoke only in my head. Sort of head–to–head conversation. My ancestors thought he was too handsome and would be a distraction to my studies and made him shapeshift into dog form. He's handsome for sure, he's tall and tanned with blonde hair that comes to his shoulders and light brown eyes that look goldish-yellow, and he's a real English Lord, his father was an Earl."

"Right then, I would be particularly interested in meeting your friend Mick. Where is he now?"

"He's still in Ireland; he has a lot of work to do repairing the destruction caused by the fae war. He will call me every day, or I will call him, well not on the phone, just in my head. He likes to check in to see how I am and what I'm doing. He's bossy like that."

Friar Xavier laughs along with Bridget; she can feel him relaxing. The friar is easy to speak with; she tells him of her time in Dublin. About meeting the Queen of the Fae and the King of the Leprechauns, and finding out that she is their many times removed great-granddaughter.

Friar Xavier gets a good insight into Bridget's personality when she tells of Fergus and the Warriors winning the war and never mentions her part. Everyone in the Fae and Immortal realm has heard how she saved the Fae Race by asking

Mother Earth for help. He asks, "You have enjoyed meeting your new family?"

"They are wonderful. Especially Mick. Whoever knew that a dog would be such good company? Well, he is human, but I spent a great deal of time with him in dog form. He is a great friend. Meeting him as a talking dog helped. I'm not much of a talker, I guess."

Bridget doesn't notice the Friar trying hard not to laugh at her comment about not being much of a talker, as she continues speaking. "Hmm, I wonder how many dogs talk to their owners, well maybe not as much as Mick, at least, I hope not. That dog can really talk. When I found out that Mick was Lord Howth, I complained a lot about the constant chatter in my head. He went on and on with my "lessons," but here I am, with hundreds of people around, and feel sad that I have no one to share this with, well not anymore since you came along. I'm very happy to meet you, friar. Oh, sorry, should I address you as "Father," as I would a priest?"

"Friar will be fine my dear. I believe your ancestors are correct in believing that you have many gifts. You have accomplished a great deal for one so young."

"I'm not that young. I'm almost eighteen, well, actually I turned seventeen last month. Sorry, I'm talking your ear off. I guess I'm a little lonely. I should feel excited. I'm sitting in a park, only a few hundred feet from Buckingham Palace, one of the most beautiful places in the world. It would be fun to talk to Mick about the palace. I can hear him now with that snooty tone of voice, 'Bridget, Buckingham Palace has been the official residence of the British Royal family since 1837.' He can really be annoying, but I miss him."

"It must feel peculiar being alone in a foreign country," Friar Xavier asks, still trying to ascertain the full story behind her sadness.

"I felt at home in London right away. New York has a lot in common with London, like the number of people, diversity of cultures, even the subway, or underground as you call it here."

"You like our city then?"

"Yes, I love it! I've been all over. I went to a pub for lunch and checked out Harrods. Mick told me that I needed to relax and enjoy the sights, but I have a strong feeling that I need to be doing something. I guess that's what led me here to meet you. Fergus said that I might be able to help you with a problem you have?"

"Pardon me miss, may I be of assistance?"

Bridget looks up and sees a guy in a midnight blue uniform. He's wearing a helmet with an emblem on it that has a crown sitting on a badge with the letters, 'EB.' A cop or what the English call a constable is looking at her with a puzzled look on his face. She realizes that she has been talking out loud, and no one but her will be able to see or hear Friar Xavier.

"Sorry, I was just thinking out loud, everything's okay."

"Yes, miss, good day then." He touches his hand to his helmet and gives her the cop look.

I wonder if all cops go to a special school to learn that look. It makes you feel guilty even if you aren't. Now that I think about it, the nuns at school had that look down pat. She waits until the constable walks away and then turns back to Friar Xavier. "I'm sorry if I'm talking too much."

"Not at all my dear, please continue."

"The last time I was here with Fergus, I had a strange feeling. I felt I was needed, not then, but soon. Sounds strange, doesn't it? The other reason is that I have a cousin that lives here in England. He's one of the other reasons I came to London. I have to find someone to take over the land that I inherited in Ireland. I know they all think I will spend the rest of my life at the palace or fix up the farm, but that's not me. I would prefer to find someone in the Kerins family, who would love the land and take good care of it. You see, there is a faeire mound on the land that must not be disturbed, so I have to make sure that whoever takes over the land believes that there is magic in the world."

Friar Xavier nods his head and quietly listens. Now he understands Bridget's sadness. He wonders why she feels she needs to leave her fae family.

"This past month I had a knowing. I don't quite understand it myself, but somehow I knew that there was another human Kerins out there somewhere. I finally found a cousin, with Google's help, but his home answering machine has a message that says, he's out of town and not due back for a couple of days. So I'm just playing tourist. I'm glad you're here; I will be happy to help you any way I can."

Bridget spots a couple who have stopped a few feet away and are looking at her. They see a young girl sitting on a bench, in the rain, talking out loud. Before they call the constable or a shrink, Bridget turns back to Friar Xavier and asks with her new head-talk skill, "Friar is it okay if we speak with our thoughts only?" She nods in the direction of the couple. "It might be less conspicuous, and I love using my fae talent."

At that moment, the young fae are gathering at Stonehenge.

Chapter 3

Stonehenge
Amesbury, England

As the air stilled, the firelight drew giant shadows beneath the stones, which stand guard north of the small town of Amesbury, in Salisbury Plain. The sound of neither voice nor wing could be heard as the eldest opened the gold lined wood case that held the prophecy.

Over a hundred strong, they held their breath. Anxious to hear again the prophecy that brought the American to Ireland to save all fae.

Emanon read the words of comfort. "It has been written that when the darkness swells to encompass all that lies before it, one who is not of our land but who is of royal blood will come to learn, to battle, to stop the evil from spreading throughout the world."

"And she did!" The usually quiet Leonda cries out. Embarrassed now at her outburst, she turns to her friend and whispers, "Que-tip; she did save us, right?"

"Of course, she did, now it is time you stop worrying about the future. Live in the here and now like I do." Que-tip flips her pink sparkled wing at her friend, and nose bumps her until Leonda giggles.

Que-tip looks around at the young fae and realizes that they are still frightened from too many years of fearing Morrigan and her evil creatures. Que-tip wonders if there is something she can do to help them feel safer. She has heard that Bridget was in England; maybe she could get her to come to Stonehenge. If they meet her, and she tells them they are safe, maybe then they will let go of their fear. Que-tip pats her hair back in place and flies off.

Chapter 4

St. James Park
London, England

"Am I to understand that you may have some time on your hands at the moment? Would it be too presumptuous of me to ask for your assistance?"

"Of course not Friar, I would love to help you with anything," Bridget answers telepathically, not wanting to draw too much attention to herself.

"Now, this is a blessing. I was praying that someone could help. My role is to keep the royal family content. I am their unseen counselor and can often aid them without their knowing. But this latest problem has me very worried for our dear Queen's health, very worried indeed."

"What problem?"

"Have you read of the dog napping at the Queen's home in Sandringham?"

"Yes, it's in all the papers. It's so sad; I don't understand how folks can be so cruel. I heard they want some jewels. The

Queen is worth millions. Can't she just give them the jewels and get her dogs back?"

"That is not her way. She will not bow down to the threats of criminals. Be that as it may, the jewels they want are not hers to give. They belong to the people. The ransom note specified the Crown Jewels."

"I'm was planning on seeing them. The Crown Jewels are on display at the Tower of London, aren't they?"

"Yes, you see, that is also part of this puzzle. On one hand, to take the dogs without being caught was clever. To ask a ransom of something that the Queen cannot give, now that would make the persons who absconded with the Queen's dogs not very clever, or very, very clever indeed, do you see my problem?"

"Yes, I do," Bridget answers amazed at the Friar's mixture of old language, and modern day terms.

"Is that what you were doing just now, listening to those two gentlemen to see if you could find more clues?"

"Correct, and it is as bad as I thought. People are all pointing fingers at the

French for causing this disaster. But that makes no sense. Why would one country want to cause unrest in another country, over something so insignificant to the world at large?"

Her favorite subject in school is history and is amazed at the smallest things that can trigger a war.

Bridget reminds Friar Xavier, "Well, it has been done many times in the past over things just as insignificant."

"Sadly, you are correct," he says as he shakes his head from side to side, not wanting to accept the stupidity of man.

"Perhaps I can help, I'm not doing anything right now. What have you learned about the case so far?"

"I know that everyone is working on it, and this little matter has the world's attention. The result is always the same. They seem to believe that the young French girl who was the veterinary assistant was the inside contact."

"They have to have some evidence to come up with that opinion. Do you know what it is?"

"The information I have is that Michelle was hired recently. She is the daughter of an English father and French mother who divorced when she was young. She was raised in France but would come over often to visit her father and assist him in his veterinary practice. She is attending the Royal Veterinary College part time, working on her degree in veterinary medicine. The men I was listening to are with MI5, they were saying that she is under surveillance and is now sitting on the steps of The Wedding Cake."

"The wedding cake?"

"Quite so," the Friar smiles, lighting up his face and bringing a twinkle to his eyes. "Queen Mum's Memorial is nicknamed, "The Wedding Cake" as it represents the decoration on the top of one. In fact, if you get into a black cab, and ask to be taken to "The Wedding Cake" many drivers will automatically take you here to the Victoria Memorial. It is just up ahead. Have you been that direction yet?"

"No, actually, I was about to see Buckingham Palace, and now I have someone to share it with."

"It is a fine day for a bit of a walk. If you would like my, how shall I say, limited company? I would enjoy accompanying you and let you know a little of the story of The Wedding Cake. I so enjoyed watching it being built."

"Lead on Macduff," Bridget says as she stands.

"Actually my name is..... Oh yes, Willie does have a few catchy phrases now doesn't he."

Wow, he calls Shakespeare, 'Willie,' what better company than one who has witnessed so much history. Here I was beginning to get bored, and now I have another adventure. What is it that Mick would say? "Life is an adventure! Carpe Diem. Seize the day!"

Friar Xavier walks beside Bridget and begins to tell her some bits and pieces of the history of the area. "In recent years, much of the area around the Memorial has been made ready for pedestrians. From the steps of the Victoria Memorial, you get great views. It was built in the time when Rule Britannia was a reality and follows a nautical theme."

"I can't wait to see it."

"I will soon show you."

It sounds that, unlike Mick, this guy enjoys playing teacher. Or it could be that he's also lonely, and likes talking to someone.

"Friar, how is it that you can travel about? From all I have read, spirits stay where their body is buried, of course, that is the human's view of things." Bridget laughs.

"Actually, one, such as I, feels comfortable visiting those places that one visited most often. We are not limited at all. We may show up anywhere we choose. I am lucky in that, as a Friar, who was in Royal favor, I visited many of the palaces in the area. William the Conqueror bequeathed the site that Buckingham Palace is built on to the monks of Westminster Abbey. Sandringham and Hampton Court were also sites of monasteries at one time. You must visit Hampton Court Palace. It is the home of a very good friend of mine, Skeletor. He is quite famous. You might have heard of him?"

"Skeletor? No, I don't believe so. Why is he famous?"

"My friend is the famed CCTV ghost. 'Skeletor' is the name that was given to him after he appeared on a CCTV camera at Hampton Court Palace in October 2003," he chuckles.

"Can you do that, just appear at will?"

With his blue eyes sparkling and a huge smile he explains. "Once in a great while, but the emotions have to warrant it. His emotions were very strong that day. It seems that a great many strangers were mucking about. He kept opening the door, and they kept closing it. He lost his temper and appeared to scare them off. Since that fateful day, many more visitors have come to Hampton Court Palace in hopes of catching a glimpse of the ghost."

"Poor Skeletor," Bridget giggles.

As they walk closer to the palace, Bridget can see parts of it through the trees. Friar Xavier continues his lecture, and she finds that she enjoys listening to him. When they leave the shelter of the trees, she can see a large crowd of people.

"Go on up the steps of The Wedding Cake for the best view," her new found friend and guide advises. "I need to pop in to check on the Queen."

Bridget can hardly believe she is standing on the steps of Queen Mum's Memorial in front of Buckingham Palace watching a ghost fly over the people and into the palace.

There are at least a hundred people in the area, most standing at the twenty foot tall, black, wrought iron rail. They all have cameras or cell phones pointed at the two guards as they exchange places with two new ones. Standing on the steps, Bridget has a great view. She stands there in silence and gives thanks that she has this opportunity.

Her companion of the last twenty minutes returns. She sees him float down into the crowd. She looks around and sees him sitting on a step, next to an extremely thin girl. Her short cut burgundy tinted hair is streaked with black. Bridget can't see her face; it's buried in her hands. Her shoulders are shaking as if she is crying. No one but Friar Xavier is sitting close to her. *I guess people think if they get too close her sadness will intrude on their joy.*

Bridget goes over and sits down next to her. The stone step is damp and cold. She reaches into her satchel and turns to the sad girl, "would you like a Kleenex?"

Startled, the girl looks up, and Bridget can see what might be a beautiful face if it wasn't tear-stained and blotchy. Her eyes are red-rimmed, and her nose is bright red. She looks as if she's been crying a long time. Bridget hands her the small tissue pack she always carries.

Bridget takes this opportunity to check her out as Mick has taught her to do. Mick explained that everyone gives off an energy signal. As one learns to read it, the signal will tell more about a person than you can gather from just speaking with them. The sad girl has an aura that is mostly dark green and charcoal gray, which, according to Mick, shows she's depressed with mental stress. Mostly her aura is the aqua color of a healer and salmon pink, showing she has found her true vocation. The aura reading and Bridget's gut tell her all that she needs to know. She tells the Friar. *Michelle is innocent. She did not take the dogs. I sure hope MI5 has more suspects.*

"Merci," the girl says as she takes one tissue and returns the package.

"Is there anything that I can do to help?" Bridget asks.

"No, thank you. The Dorgis are missing," the girl cries.

"Doggies?"

"No no, my petite four Dorgis, my little Cider, Berry, Candy, and Vulcan, but you know nothing; you are American!"

"Yes, I'm American. We do read the newspapers. Are you referring to the Queen's dogs that were taken from her home, what's it called? Oh yes, Sandringham House."

"Oui, ah yes, pardon. I do not mean to offend. Most tourists are too busy having fun to watch the news broadcasts or read the paper. I am, or should I say, was, the Queen's assistant veterinary at Sandringham House in charge of the Dorgis."

"Sounds like a great job."

"It was. The Queen has a Corgi named Susan from whom she bred numerous successive dogs. Some Corgis mated with dachshunds. Most notably the Corgi named Pipkin, who belonged to Princess Margaret, to create 'Dorgis.' The Dorgis are her pride and joy; they are ce Magnifique." She buries her head in her hands again and continues to cry.

"Could you tell me what happened. I really do want to help if I can." Bridget is worried that she won't stop crying long enough for her to learn all she needs to help find the pups.

She lifts her head and looks at Bridget, sniffles, blows her nose and says, "The Queen has entertained many a noted breeder at her home. It was during one of these 'showings' or how you would say, 'garden parties for dogs,' that someone took the Dorgis. They think I am that someone."

"But why does everyone think you are to blame?"

"I was called to the phone and left the Dorgis alone. They were safe in their cages in the old lodge. When I picked up the phone, no one was on it. I looked around for the man who gave me the message, but he was not to be found. I search everywhere for him. He said my mother was on the phone, and I wanted to know if she left him a message. You see, she is traveling in Africa, and I cannot call her back. My father, he died last year. She is the only one whom I can speak to about all this, and I cannot reach her."

Before she starts crying again, Bridget asks more questions. "Were there other dog handlers in the old lodge when you left to answer the phone?"

"No, they were busy at the new kennel, it just opened this week. Everything is state of the art, all, what you say, hi-tech. The same man who gave me the message to answer the phone at the main house was the man who told me that the Queen wanted her petites for a private showing. He was wearing a badge as a judge, and I did not question him."

"So you didn't question a private showing at the old kennel?"

"No, the Queen has done that many times in the past. The old kennel is still set up for showings. It is not scheduled to be torn down until later this week. What does this all matter, they are gone," she cries.

Bridget hands her another tissue. "My name is Bridget, and I'd like to help you if there is anything I can do. What is your name?"

"Ah Oui, my name is Michelle Beaulieu, what was your name?" She asks, turning to look at the blonde girl with the sea green eyes, holding a funny red and white umbrella.

Royal Dorgis

"I'm Bridget."

"Bridgette is a beautiful French name," Michelle says.

Bridget loves how Michelle pronounces her name. "It is a Gaelic name. My family came from Ireland. I come from the States."

"Oui, I can tell your accent."

"I'm sorry you are having problems; perhaps I can help?"

"No, it is I that is sorry for all the tears. I am asked to leave my post. This insufferable inspector, he tells me I am suspicious."

"You mean a suspect? They think you stole the puppies?"

"I didn't know where to go. I guess I am sitting here, wanting to see the Queen and let her know that I am innocent. She is a good lady. I know. Only good lady loves her Dorgis so much. They will not let me in." She nods in the direction of the Queen's guards. "I have been trying all morning to see her. I know she is in there, see the pendant, it is flying. That means that she is here, but she will not see me. To her, I am suspicious also." Michelle places her face in her hands and cries again.

Yikes! I thought I was a watering pot when I was in Ireland, but I couldn't have been this bad. Bridget takes another tissue from the pack and hands it to her. "Here, the best thing to do is to dry your face and let's go someplace dry and have something to eat." Even with her raincoat and umbrella, Bridget feels damp. Sitting on a cold, wet, stone step doesn't help.

She gets no response from Michelle and tries again. "I'm starving, how about you?" Bridget stands up and waits for Michelle to join her, she doesn't move.

Bridget looks up at Friar Xavier hovering above, and he nods encouragingly and tells her, *"Please keep trying, she will get sick sitting out here."*

She tries again, "Hey Michelle, whenever I have a problem, I know that any action is better than sitting still and worrying. Come on, let's go."

Finally, Michelle stands to join her, and they head to the line of taxis next to the street entrance. Happy to be doing something, Bridget asks, "How would you like a pub lunch?"

Michelle looks a little dazed but shakes her head in the affirmative. Bridget waves at a black cab and asks him to take them to a local pub for lunch. Michelle may have thought it a little strange that Bridget held the cab door open a little longer than usual, as she waits for Friar Xavier to have a seat next to her before she joins them. *I think this ride will be a fun experience for the friendly Friar.*

Bridget's in luck. The cab drops them off within ten minutes, so the ride didn't cost too much. They are in front of a large two-story pub. Bridget learned in Ireland that the best food could be found in the pubs, and they are open to all ages. A pub is more like a family gathering place than a bar in the states. Looking at the pub, she would say it was well over a hundred years old. No flashy signs, just a discreet old wooden sign above the door reads 'Thrasher Pub' in weathered, bright colored paint. If it weren't for the sign, you would think that this was someone's home. She heard in New York to always trust a cabbie to know the best places to eat.

Bridget opens the large wooden door, darkened with age, to a color scheme of deep burgundies, browns, mustards and dark blues that blend to give that great old English pub look she read about in the tourist guides. There are various seating options including leather sofas or chairs. Along one long mirrored wall is a wooden bar with a brass rail and bar stools. The host greets them with menus in hand, dressed in a colorful vest and tie that work well with the surroundings. Bridget thinks he asks them to follow him, but sometimes when the accent is strong, she is never quite sure. He first shows them to a couple of leather chairs in front of the fireplace, but she asks for a booth she spots in the back. She wants to sit in an area that is a little more private, in case Michelle loses it again.

Bridget looks over at Michelle, and she's checking out the old English decor. She looks at Friar Xavier and burst out laughing. The good Friar is in mid-air staring at the large glass canisters of pickled eggs and what she hopes isn't pig's feet. *I don't think spirits eat, or I would order some for him.* Michelle looks to see what she is laughing at and only sees the old time memorabilia on the walls.

"Let's get a seat," Bridget says as they follow the host. They both read the menu and soon a waitress in a dress that looks like it's straight from a Hollywood costume shop and is intended for women who worked in pubs in the nineteen century. It has a full, dark green billowing skirt and a beige top that reminds Bridget of a peasant blouse that shows way too much skin. She smiles as she comes over to take their order. The menu includes the history of the pub and a write-up on how they use farm fresh products including locally raised beef. That sounded good, and they both order cheeseburgers. Bridget orders a Diet Coke and Michelle, who looks ninety pounds soaking wet orders a milkshake. *I'll never understand some people; they can eat anything and not gain weight.* Bridget grumbles to herself.

While they wait for the food, they look around at all the great paintings of medieval England and some village scenes with musicians. Bridget is grateful there are no paintings of dogs.

When the food arrives, Bridget realizes she is starving. She is halfway through her burger when she notices that Michelle is using a knife and fork to cut her burger into itsy bitsy little pieces before she eats it. *Wow, that's strange, but it may be why she's so thin.*

Michelle has a fashion model look. Her mahogany hair has a very expensive cut that emphasizes the pixie-like features of her face. Even with the dark circles under eyes that are red rimmed from crying, she is beautiful.

When Michelle removes her very fashionable raincoat, Bridget thinks she is looking at a style fresh from Vogue magazine. Michelle is wearing a beautifully tailored, bold black and red plaid patterned, light wool suit with large bright red buttons, a black purse, and black patent leather boots with red bows. Bridget realizes that Michelle dressed to meet with the Queen, but suspects she would look well dressed in whatever she wore. Bridget loves clothes, but her vintage Pendleton herringbone jacket and jeans can't compare to Michelle's outfit. *It must be a French number; I have never seen anything like it.*

Bridget watches Michelle in amazement; she even makes eating look like art. *Whoever heard of someone eating a cheeseburger with a fork and knife?* She cuts a small piece of a cheeseburger, puts down her fork and knife, then picks up her fork, places a tiny piece in her mouth. Puts down the fork chews for so long you would think she has half of the burger in her mouth instead of a piece that would get lost on a teaspoon. Then she waits a minute or so before she starts the process over again.

Michelle looks as if she loves every bite and doesn't say a word the whole time she is eating. Bridget looks down at her half-finished burger and the remaining ten percent of her fries and realizes that Michelle may be onto something. It looks like she is enjoying her food and Bridget eats so fast, she doesn't remember taking the time to taste. Michelle is sure taking the time to enjoy every tiny bite. Bridget starts to pick up a fork but feels foolish. She grabs her Coke and continues to watch Michelle.

When she finishes about a quarter of her burger and just a few of the fries, Michelle pushes her plate away and says, "That was very good, thank you for bringing me here. I was very hungry."

"You're welcome; I'm happy you like it."

"Are you on holiday here in London?"

"Yes, sort of a working vacation, I inherited farmland in Ireland that I would love to see go to a relative. I learned I have a cousin here in London, but he's out of town at the moment, so I get to play. Hopefully, he would like to move to Ireland and take care of the farm. I know nothing about farming, and I need to get home to Brooklyn. I guess."

"It does not sound as if you are very anxious to get home, but if you need help in seeing the sights, I could help you do that."

"Could you? That would be great. I've asked a few folks where to go, but I couldn't understand a word they said. I think they were speaking English, but the accent was different."

"You must have spoken to persons with a Cockney accent. It does cause one to listen very hard. It is a rhyming slang," Michelle explains.

Bridget looks next to her where Friar Xavier is sitting and sees him shake his head. She gives herself a mental head slap and says, "Actually instead of sightseeing, I would like to help you out if I can. Maybe we could go to Sandringham House and look around; you never know what we may find."

"You meant it; you want to help me?"

"Sure, why not. I can tell that you didn't steal those dogs. You don't look much like "Cruella De Vil.""

Michelle has a puzzled look.

"I guess you've never seen '101 Dalmatians' huh, don't know what you're missing. I love all the Disney shows," Bridget explains.

"Ah Oui, she was the evil doggie nipper," she laughs briefly, "As if I could ever be an evil doggie nipper, I love my little Dorgis," and begins to cry again. "It is no good; there is no help for me," Michelle sobs.

"Don't give up, let's just go there and try."

"You don't understand. I am not allowed anywhere near Sandringham or the Dorgis ever again."

"Oh, I forgot about that. We will think of someplace nearby to hide you."

Bridget pays the check and the tip; surprised Michelle didn't offer to help out. *Oh well, I invited her, and she's out of work at present. I have money now. I can afford lunch.*

They put on their rain gear, open the large front door, and walk out into a downpour.

"Wow, now this is rain. I guess there is no trip to the country today," Bridget announces and pulls Michelle back into the pub. "It's okay we can call a cab."

Michelle stands close and looks at her for a moment and asks "How old are you, Bridgette?"

Shocked, Bridget doesn't answer the question right away, Michelle takes her chin in her hand, "What age?"

If she tries to pry my mouth open to check my teeth, I'm going to belt her one. Bridget backs away and says, "Seventeen, why what's up?"

"Old skin, you do not take good care of yourself. We go to the spa and get pampered. What do you say? You need a facial for the old skin."

"Old skin, what the heck...."

But Michelle's no longer there to argue with. Next thing Bridget knows she is being pulled back out into the downpour. She watches Michelle hail a cab and gives the address to the driver. *I guess I am on the way to get treatment for my old skin.*

Bridget looks over at a smiling Friar Xavier. He telepathically tells her, *"I will return to the palace and check back with you in a couple of days."* A few shimmers and he is gone.

"Great, no help from him, I guess his travel adventure doesn't include a beauty spa," Bridget mumbles.

Chapter 5

Bellisa Spa
London's East End

They exit the cab and run to two large glass doors. Bridget is surprised when two women dressed in severe black maid uniforms meet them and hand her a fluffy white towel. Michelle speaks to them in French, then turns to her and says with a broad smile, "Bridgette finish drying; they will make room for us."

Michelle has already reached the second floor, and Bridget hurries to catch up. She almost trips up the steps as she tries to take in the crystal chandelier and elegant surroundings. *Wow, this is a spa?*

Bridget realizes that folks respond to stress in different ways. She guesses Michelle's idea of dealing with a charge of dog-napping and the loss of her job is to spend money at a spa.

Before she knows what's happening, Michelle's gone. She's led to a dressing room and handed a robe made of the same extra thick white terry cloth as the towels. *What on earth? They are giving me a facial right? Why do I need a dressing room and a robe?*

"Are you ready?"

Bridget opens the door to tell Michelle to *forgetaboutit.* Michelle stands in front of her door; she is all in white; her hair covered in a white turban, she is wearing fuzzy white scruffs and matching robe. All that is noticeable is her big smile.

Darn, she looks happy. Okay, I guess I can do this, "I'll be right there." Bridget closes the door and hurries to get out of her wet clothes.

Bridget is led to a room that looks like the inside of a bottle of Pepto Bismal it's all pink with white trim. The woman, whose name tag reads, Audrey, puts a hot fluffy, lavender scented white washcloth on her face. She quickly closes her eyes before she is sick on pink, then takes a deep breath and begins to relax as Audrey removes the cloth and softly lathers her with creams. The air smells like lavender, and she is ready to fall asleep when another washcloth, this time, ice cold, is placed on her face and vigorously rubbed. Now wide awake, Audrey says something in French and gestures for her to follow her to another room.

The new room is different, no pink. Everything in this room is white and black. Bridget is shown to an area with two large white leather armchairs that are sitting on black pedestals. In front of the chairs are white mini hot tubs, in front of the hot tubs are stools only a couple of feet off the ground.

Audrey gestures to her to have a seat just as Michelle comes into the room. "How did you like your facial, wasn't it heaven?"

"It was an adventure. Thank you, but what's with the chair."

"One must have a pedicure on a day like this," Michelle giggles.

"But I never..."

"Sit. Put your feet in the tub; you will love it." Says a short little, barrel-shaped lady whose name tag read, Doris.

Bridget did as instructed and then realizes why the chair is so big and well-constructed. The dang water is so hot that she screams and pushes back. She would have tumbled over in a smaller chair. She pulls her poor feet out of the tub of water; they are beet red.

"You will adjust to the temperature. Put your feet back in," says the spa Nazi, in a commanding voice. Bridget looks over at Michelle for help, and she is still smiling. *Maybe she did take the dogs; she has a mean streak.*

After a few minutes, Bridget has to agree that Michelle is correct, and her poor red feet adjust to the heat. Doris who is also wearing a black dress with a white apron hands them each a flute of clear sparkling liquid.

Bridget thanks her and turns to Michelle, "What's this?"

"It is the champagne, of course, a good year," she says with approval, looking at the date on the bottle left on a little black glass table between them. "It is wonderful Bridgette, drink up."

Bridget starts relaxing and thinks about how much she will tell her former neighbor, Mrs. Miller, the next time she writes. She couldn't tell her about the leprechauns and faeire, but she will get a great laugh at her, of all people, drinking champagne and getting treatments in a spa.

"I'm glad I came along Michelle, thank you so much, this is a once in a lifetime experience, it sure beats being a tourist by myself."

She takes a sip of the 'wonderful' champagne and tries not to grimace. *Champagne is way overrated. It tastes like diet ginger ale.*

She looks over at Michelle and admits that the facial helped, her face looks great, and she seems much more relaxed.

Michelle notices Bridget looking at her and giggles. She reaches over to play with the buttons on Bridget's chair.

"What are you doing?"

"These chairs are 'Ce Magnifique!' You will see."

Soon the chair begins to heat up and what feels like metal balls begin to move up and down her spine. "Wow that does feel wonderful," Bridget admits.

Now if she wasn't so embarrassed by having a woman, much older than her sitting on a low stool in front of the wash basin, picking up her foot and washing it. *OH MY GOSH, I forgot to shave!!* Hoping no one will notice she asks the foot lady to pronounce her name. *That's it, lady, please look at my face while we talk and don't notice my hairy legs.*

Of course, the woman ignores her and puts white cream all over her leg, and all the tiny stubs of hair now look an inch long. The black hairs stand up like soldiers at attention. Bridget just wants to die. She keeps trying to get her leg out of the woman's hands and back into the water, but Doris holds on like a pit bull.

The heck with it, I'm paying for this madness. Why should I allow anyone to embarrass me?

Bridget pours herself a full glass of champagne and begins to enjoy the experience. That's until the water demon starts to use a block of sandpaper on the bottom of her foot, she jumps so high, not only does she spill the champagne but the flute goes flying and crashes against a fancy glass case. The chair falls over backward and Bridget lands on the ground. The tub of water spills over Doris.

Several women, all in black come running and yelling in French.

Michelle is right behind her when they leave the French spa. She is crying again. "I'm so sorry Michelle, I didn't mean to embarrass you. I paid for the damage."

"It is not you, my friend. When they ran my credit card and noticed my name, they told me that I am an embarrassment to all France, and I would never be welcomed in their establishment again."

Bridget puts her arm through hers, and they walk down the fresh rain-washed street. "Hey girlfriend, at those prices, you can hire yourself a full-time maid."

Michelle doesn't laugh as Bridget hoped, so she picks up an empty Coke can off the street and backhands it into the corner trash bin. When it misses, she gives it a puzzled look, "Darn, it worked with a champagne flute."

Michelle looks at Bridget's serious face and bursts out laughing. "You Americans, you are crazy in the head."

"You may be right, but that's what makes us lovable."

They both laugh and talk about Bridget's first spa experience. As they walk, they plan their trip to the Queen's home in the country for the following morning.

As they approach the underground subway station, Bridget feels something's not right. The hairs stand up on the back of her neck. She feels she is being watched, she looks around but doesn't see anyone. She takes a deep breath and realizes why she feels so spooked; whatever is watching them is not friendly, and certainly not human.

Chapter 6

Bridget's Apartment
Battersea, England

Bridget waves goodbye to Michelle and laughs as she yells "Cheerio." With her strong French accent, it sounds more like Sheri-O. She waits until Michelle hails a cab for her trip home, then walks down the well-lit stairs to enter the tube station for her 30 minute trip to Battersea.

Her timing's terrible, the station's packed. Luckily she doesn't have to wait too long because the trains run every fifteen minutes. No one seems to be paying her any attention, but she still has a feeling of being watched. She has put up with crowded platforms and eccentric folks for most of her life; it doesn't mean she likes it.

Bridget's stay in Ireland opened her eyes to another world. It is so very different than Brooklyn, New York. Being a city girl born and raised, she can't believe she fell in love with country living in such a short time. Well if she was honest, not only did she fall in love with the country. It was her family and Mick. She has to admit that she will miss not only her fae family but everyone else, especially Mick. *Okay, stop feeling sorry for yourself, you know you couldn't stay with Mick, geese he is like over a hundred years older than you.*

It's a pain to wait for trains and buses, too much time to think. She would much rather drive than take a train, but parking in London is a major hassle. *How am I going to face a future without Mick and my fae family? Okay, let go of the fear, the future will take care of itself.*

Bridget shakes her head as if that would stop her thinking of Mick. She looks around the crowded platform. Mick is not the only one that taught her always to be aware of her surroundings. Growing up in the hood is a major lesson in survival. Fear will only get in the way she reminds herself. With her newfound skill, she reaches out to see if she can pinpoint the source of her current unease. There it is, on the bench, not a shadow but the absence of one. Like a blank space where there shouldn't be one. *I wonder what evil creature can be invisible; I will need to check with Mick.* She walks over and says, "Be gone with ye now and don't come back."

It's gone, thank goodness her mother's old saying works. In Ireland, she didn't feel this fear. She wonders what has changed.

"Your awareness of the seen and unseen will one day rescue you from a depth of pain you could never have imagined. Trust with your heart." The odd whispery words from an unknown female float over Bridget sending a shiver down her spine. She takes some deep breaths to calm down. It isn't that she doesn't feel safe alone in train stations. *Mom always made sure I knew how to protect myself. The self-defense training she dragged me to will stay with me forever.*

Her mother passed away from cancer when she was fourteen, two years before she left the U.S. for Ireland. She remembers her lessons in self-defense. She reaches into her purse for her wallet and moves it to her jean pocket. Her keys with the mace canister attached go into her coat pocket for easy access.

The train arrives, and it's packed solid, the volume of voices high with a variety of accents. The seats are all taken, and she has to stand. As the train approaches the Trafalgar Square station, people begin to gather their belongings to switch to other train lines or to hop on a bus.

Bridget spots a seat by the window. Two rows of double seats that face each other are more comfortable than the long bench of seats with people on both sides and others standing over you. She sprints over to the recently vacated seat, sits and looks out of the window.

Riding a train is very familiar. Back home in Brooklyn, she rode a train to school and then to her job in the city. She started working at the age of twelve because they needed the money. Her father passed away when she was little, and her mother's illness was keeping her in bed most of the time, money was tight. Her mother still insisted Bridget enjoy after school activities. Her mother didn't know about her job after school, as a hat check girl at the New York Coliseum, but approved of her working weekends at Mrs.

Slotnick's bakery near her home on Washington Avenue.

She begins to relax and finds herself taking deep breaths, as her friend the Selkie taught her at Howth Castle in Scotland. She looks out at the darkness of the tunnels as they race by and lets her mind drift.

The tunnels are a city beneath the city, a world of their own. In a strange way, the movement has a mesmerizing effect and Bridget soon begins to yawn. *I don't know why I'm so tired. Maybe it's because the day started early with a friendly ghost and then a French nut case whom I feel connected with, I wonder why. Michelle is rude, a little arrogant and an 'in your face' personality. Hey, she could be a New Yorker.*

Maybe it's the same with all folks from large cities. We have our unique identity and don't see anything wrong with it. She does push it a little, like that 'old skin' comment, what's with that? I'm glad we stopped for tea somewhere quiet; she's really upset.

Bridget doesn't believe Michelle would hurt a flea. She doesn't understand why everyone is blaming her and wonders what evidence they have.

How on earth is she going to help her? Well no matter, it's more fun than waiting for her cousin Peter to get back from his holiday. Glad they had a nice long talk about Sandringham, how things work, what her job was. A lot of things are beginning to make more sense.

More awake now, Bridget pulls out her notebook to record all that has happened today. She is finding it hard to believe it was just a few hours ago that she met Friar Xavier and wound-up promising that she will go to Sandringham tomorrow and see what could have happened to the Dorgis.

She doesn't think Michelle will be much help; she's way too upset. The major problem is, who took the Dorgis and why do they want to frame her. Bridget adds to her list:

What does this place look like?

What evidence does the police have? It must be something good for them to tell her not to leave the country. Can't be too bad or they would've put her behind bars already.

Michelle was so upset that the manager of the spa asked her not to return. Did her countrywomen suspect her or they just don't like the bad press? Think it will hurt business? Whatever happened to innocent until proven guilty? Or is that just in America? Well, even there people tend to believe all that they hear on TV or read in the newspapers.

Bridget closes her eyes and listens to the sounds around her as the train continues racing towards Battersea. The crowds are beginning to thin out. The sound of the conductor calling out, *"Mind the Gap"* is the only difference between a New York City subway and the tube. A man enters the train and sits next to her. He opens his newspaper; her mind continues to wander as she hears folks getting off to go home.

Mick would say *'Carpe Deme'* seize the day... enjoy each minute. She opens her eyes and looks again at her notebook. The page has flipped back to her list from yesterday, she reads, '#1, Meet with Peter to see if he would like to take over the land.'

That's certainly still her priority, but can she keep busy while she waits? When she made her decision to leave, she promised herself that the very first thing she must do is to find a relative to take over the land in Ireland. It can't go out of the family, and her fae family needs a human to interact with the locals. She can't imagine her family land sold to a developer. What if they built a McDonald's on it? She would be haunted the rest of her life and beyond. Imagine if they tried to move the faeire mound, all sorts of bad luck might befall them. Hmm, she wonders how her new family would like haunting an old apartment building in Brooklyn. She knows some of the tenants wouldn't notice anything different about them. She chuckles.

Guess there's a lot she doesn't know about spirits. Her great, many, times removed, great-grandmother might be Geraldine the Queen of the Faeire, but she's not very highfalutin for a queen. She had to smile when the Queen said "call me Grace," and her old granddad "Padraig." For the King of the Leprechauns, is a funny character. She wonders if they can leave the land in Ireland or are they trapped there because their bodies are buried there.

They have been so wonderful; she will miss them. How does she explain that she doesn't want to be trapped? That she doesn't want to live in the palace, she wants to travel and see the world. *Who am I kidding, I don't feel trapped, and I don't want to see the world alone, if only Mick... Okay, don't go down that road, think of something else, anything else.*

Think of ghosts. Well, she is going to learn a lot more about ghosts. At least, they don't need passports, she chuckles.

The guy next to her turns and smiles, "Here you go Luv, have a look-see," he gets up to leave and hands her the paper he'd been reading.

Oops, he must think I was reading over his shoulder and read something funny, "Ah, thanks that'll be great," She calls out after him.

She holds the paper for a second and watches as he leaves the train. Nice guy. She turns the London Times to the front page and reads the headlines. "French

Connection Proven" *GOOD GRIEF, a warrant has been issued for Michelle!*

The news article states that the authorities say Michelle can't be located. They expect that she may have left the country. *Noooo, we were in a spa, boy these news guys love to make up news. I guess exciting assumptions sell newspapers.*

Bridget wonders what to do? She can't do anything about Michelle; she is probably in the hands of the police right now. The only thing she can do is to find the Dorgis.

She looks up as a tall, slender lady, possibly in her forties, moves from her seat across the aisle to sit in the seat facing her. She looks very attractive in a vintage black overcoat with gray fur on the collar and cuffs. *Wow, that vintage coat must have cost a mint. I think that's real chinchilla.* The stranger's blonde hair is done up in a French twist and a much sought after, vintage box hat with a peek-a- boo veil, sits at a cocky angle to give her a jaunty appearance. She leans towards Bridget and says, "I couldn't help seeing the headlines, what do they think of the French in the states?"

Bridget looks at the lady who sits back in the seat, takes out her knitting, finds the spot where she stopped and looked back up at her expectantly, waiting for her answer.

"I don't hear very much about them. We love all things, French. They're still the final word in fashion. The French men you see on television are always so sexy, what's not to like?" Bridget laughs.

The stranger smiles back at Bridget, returns to her knitting and says, "I am very familiar with the French people. The Americans and English do not understand them. The French say that Americans smile all of the time, for them, there must be a reason to smile. 'Someone who smiles all the time is not to be trusted.' For them, it is hard to understand. They do not have much to smile about. Our countries do not constantly worry about invasion. For more than two thousand years the French have been invaded by one country or another. So they are wary of strangers.

"I may have been born in Florence, Italy, but I am a true Englishwoman, who has seen her share of war. Yes, one should be very wary of strangers."

Bridget is enjoying this strange lady. "I guess most folks do not understand the French people. Heck, most folks don't understand us New Yorkers."

The stranger nods her head in agreement. "New Yorkers have very strong personalities; they are very outgoing. French people are not overly outgoing. They like to take their time to get to know you. They do not understand a stranger shouting, "Hey mister, where's the Eifel Tower?" To them it is rude. Even in an emergency one is taught to be polite. One says 'Excusez-Moi de vous d'eranger madam,' which simply means 'excuse me for disturbing you madam.' Then ask your question."

Bridget smiles, "But that's not our way, New Yorkers are more direct. We are usually in a rush and want to get answers quickly. Maybe that's why folks who don't understand us call us rude."

The stranger looks up from her knitting and stares at Bridget for a second. The look in her silver-blue eyes is so piercing; it feels as if they are performing a Vulcan mind meld. Then she nods her head as if accepting what Bridget said. "The French have 2,000 years of history that have made them mistrustful of strangers. It should be *mandatory* for all government officials to learn history. We should all learn from our mistakes."

Bridget looks up as the train slows and realizes that this is her stop. "I wish I didn't have to get off; it was a pleasure speaking with you. Bye."

She races to the door, but before it closes, she hears the stranger say, "You are welcome Bridget, always question until you find the answer that feels right for you. Good luck with your search."

A stunned Bridget steps off the train to the loud announcement to "Mind the Gap." She turns and looks back, to wave at her traveling companion, but she is *gone.*

Hey, she called me by name. Who was that, was she another spirit? Bridget would have loved to talk to her for hours.

Lost in thought, she stares at the retreating train and all of a sudden she feels her skin crawl. Something evil is close. Unexpectedly, two hands push against her back, and she's flying towards the train tracks. From the corner of her eye, she sees another train approaching. She's going to die; she forgets all of her magic. The only thing she can think about is that she never got to save the Queen's Dorgis.

Suddenly she feels a sharp tug on her raincoat, and two strong hands pull her back to the platform. She sits on the ground shaking.

"Aw, you right then Miss? Want me to call someone for you?"

Bridget looks up into the eyes of a short brawny guy dressed like a construction worker. All she can do is shake her head.

"Don't be standing so close to the edge Miss; these platforms can be dangerous. Here you go then." The stranger helps her to her feet, and she finally gets out two words, "Thank you."

Chapter 7

Bridget's Apartment
Battersea, England

Bridget turns the corner onto East Street. She loves her vibrant neighborhood. Most of the buildings here were built after World War II when the Nazi bombings had destroyed most of London. The houses are mostly dark brick, three-story townhouses, and usually housing three families, one to each floor. The gardens in front hold a profusion of flowers and the many trees lining the streets help to add to the friendly atmosphere.

The absence of graffiti and sparkling windows spoke of residents that were proud of their homes. These people are looking forward, toward the future, so different from her neighborhood, where people live in fear and despair. She decides then and there that she will not return to her old neighborhood. *Maybe I can move to Jersey. I think they have affordable neighborhoods like this in Jersey.*

As she starts planning how to go about finding a budget friendly place, she sees a black cab pull up in front of the door to the apartment she has been given to use. A man steps out, closes the back door and leans in the window to hand the driver the fare. He is tall and built like a bodyguard, all muscle. He has on a dark blue shirt that's open at the collar; the cuffs rolled up on strong forearms.

Since it is no one she knows, she continues walking to the front door of her street level flat.

"Pardon me, would you be Bridget?"

"Yes, I am," she says as she turns to greet the newcomer. She immediately recognizes her cousin. Not that they look much alike. Peter looks a lot like her father, with his dark black curly hair and deep, dark brown eyes. She takes after her mother, light hair and pale skin. "Peter?"

"Yes, I'm pleased to meet you finally," he says as he stands there with his hand raised. She thinks he's undecided whether to shake her hand or give her a hug.

She rushes over and hugs him. She feels her eyes tear up. He is a blood relative. She believed, for most of her life, that she and her mother were alone. They had friends but no family. Recently, she met the family in Ireland, Geraldine and Padraig, but it's hard to hug ghosts.

"I'm so happy you are here, would you like to come in for a cup of tea?"

"I would love one. I am so sorry to come over so late. I will only stay a few minutes. I could not wait any longer to make your acquaintance."

She drops her purse and keys on the small table in the entrance hall and gestures to Peter to join her in the living room. This small, two bedroom flat was built in the "shotgun" style. One can see from the front door to the back door with the rooms all on the left side.

"I'm so happy you came over, I also couldn't wait to meet you," Bridget says as she shows him into the living room.

Peter smiles, gets a little red in the face and busies himself looking around. "This is a great flat. I have been looking for something like this. Does it come with a garden?"

"Yes, the garden is beautiful. I will enjoy it. I can see myself sitting out there and enjoying my tea in the mornings. It's a perfect location, just off the kitchen."

"Wish it was light out, I would love to see it. For tonight, the front parlor will be grand. We have so much to talk over, I should have called first, but as soon as I got home and received your message, I had to rush over."

"Have a seat. I'll put on the kettle, or would you like a Pepsi?"

"Tea would be grand."

Bridget nods and heads for the kitchen. Happy she went shopping at Harrods and bought tea and biscuits.

When she returns with the tea, Peter is looking at the large painting that takes up most of the wall. Shennum, the leprechaun captain, painted it. It shows a flower garden with pixies and faeire fluttering about.

"Nice picture isn't it?" Bridget asks, hoping he will speak of the fae folk.

"Pardon? Oh, the picture. Certainly, it is nice. Peter sits on the straight back chair across from the sofa. There is a long silence, both of them not knowing what to say. It isn't every day you get to speak with a cousin you never met. Bridget finally breaks the silence, "How was your holiday?"

"My holiday was not your typical vacation. I was working."

She waits for an uncomfortable couple of minutes and then asks, "What kind of work do you do?"

"That's a long story." Peter shakes his head and then asks, "Have you inherited any gifts from our ancestors?" He blurts out.

She thinks she knows where this was heading, but she's not sure if she's ready for it. "What kind of gifts do you mean?"

"For example, there is a strong gift of divination, of seeing the future. Some people call it intuition, I just know some things. There are millions of people with this gift, although most choose to ignore it."

Relieved, Bridget is ready to tell Peter of her recent experiences, but he continues speaking.

"When I was a kid I never knew what a strong intuition was or what it meant. Then when I got older and could read the papers, I saw a headline with a picture that could have come directly from my dreams. I was lucky that I spoke with an uncle who knew of the 'gift,' and let me know what it meant. I guess it comes to some of us in the family. A way of seeing the future, and we can decide to do something about it, or not. It is up to us."

She thought of her on-going nightmare of running away and knowing something is hunting her. She gives herself a mental kick to focus on Peter, and asks, "What kind of things have you seen over the years?"

"Well, it started out small. I would see a kid I knew crying over a lost dog, and then I would see the dog trapped in an old shed. As I got older, the demands of my gift have gotten harder. I became a private investigator to work as my cover to meet with people, and return their lost items, or rescue children, those kinds of things."

"That's fantastic. You must love your work. Now is a good time to tell you why I wanted to meet you."

Bridget tells Peter her long story about Ireland. The land she inherited, and her wish that it will be kept in the family. She skips over the fae and the war with Morrigan and how she was able to raise the dead, with the help of Mother Earth. She doesn't want to freak him out and is hoping he will get excited and volunteer to move to Ireland right away, but he is quiet and keeps looking at her under those dark, heavy eyebrows.

Anxiously she asks, "So what do you think?"

"I am glad we found one another, but I have a special job here that I must do. Ireland is not for me. Have you met any of the Irish relatives?"

Now, what do I tell him? That I met our ancestors, and they are fae? He will lock me up and throw away the key.

"I met some people, but not close relatives. I had a strong feeling that I had close family around somewhere and started checking the web."

Peter looks at her, and she feels as if he was making up his mind to tell her something extraordinary. "Have you ever been told faeire stories?"

"What kind of faeire stories?"

"This is not easy. It would be better if I knew what were your feelings were on...

well, what some people refer to as special magical gifts."

"So you know about our ancestors?" A relieved Bridget asks.

Peter moves to the edge of his seat and leans forward and asks quietly, "What do you know?"

Bridget also leans forward and inquires, "Why do you ask?"

"Before my uncle passed he spoke of a young girl that would come from overseas to save the 'Fae Race,' I had no idea what he was speaking of, but I trusted that he knew much more than he ever mentioned. I am the last of the Kerins family. I was hoping you knew something. When I saw that picture, I had a feeling I should ask you."

Bridget smiles and explains how she recently met her greats and the fae folk and how she is just learning her gifts and asks, "Do you have other gifts?"

"Not that I know of, just my one gift since childhood. Being able to see into the future is a great gift sometimes. I knew you were coming to London. I also know that you will help me stop the bombing of St. Paul's Cathedral."

"Stop the what?" Bridget jumps up and stares at Peter. "Is this another dream you know will happen? Do you know when this is going down? Will it happen soon?"

Peter rubs his hand through his hair and explains. "The dream is coming back more often; it has always been like this. When I have a dream about something of importance, and it comes to me often and then almost daily, it will happen soon; I know it. In my recent dreams, I saw you, coming from over the seas and helping me. It is strange to know that I have someone to help. I don't know what to do. I have never had this big of a challenge to deal with."

"So tell me all the details, how you see this coming down."

"I am in what looks like an abandoned tube station and there are men loading packages of C4 onto an old handcar like you see in the movies, the kind that the old miners used. Then I see St. Paul's in a million pieces."

"No! We can't let that happen! How are you going to stop it, I haven't a clue what to do, but if I can help I will try my best. Do you have any ideas?"

"I believe what I am seeing is an abandoned tube station. I have a map of all tube stations and have checked out those that are no longer in use due to repairs."

"Sounds simple enough but it will take a lot of time," Bridget says as she paces around her small living room.

"Problem is I can't locate any abandoned stations that look like the one in my dream. There is no such listing on-line, just active stations. I feel as though we don't have much time."

"Even if we find a map showing abandoned stations, we will need to narrow it down to tube stations around the cathedral. Why would someone close down a perfectly good tube station in the heart of the city?" She asks.

"I agree it doesn't make much sense."

"I'm sorry Peter; I need to head out of town for a little project, as soon as I'm done, I promise to help one hundred percent of my time."

"No problem Bridget. I will keep trying to locate the abandoned tube station that appears in my dreams."

"I will think about it also. What is your cell number? I'll call you if I think of anything."

Chapter 8

Sandringham Castle
Norfolk, England

Good thing Michelle drew her a map of the grounds last night. Michelle could have mentioned the WC on the map stood for 'water closet,' the English name for a bathroom. Bridget's thoughts wander as she leans over the salmon colored, stone sink to wash her hands. She just knew she shouldn't have had that third cup of tea. It takes forever to find a John around this huge place.

Sandringham is popular! There have to be two dozen tour buses in the parking lot. She had to park, at least, a mile away from the entrance. The Sandringham Estate is ginormous. According to the literature, it covers twenty thousand acres which include six hundred acres of woods and the County Park. The house itself is set in sixty acres of gardens. She stopped often and took pictures along the long drive from London. The Norfolk Coast region is breathtaking. She has seen many more sandy beaches than in Ireland, Hugh castles, and even a windmill. She tightens her ponytail and starts to feel she is being watched, but not by an evil presence like before. She wonders if they have a camera in the restrooms in case someone does something stupid, like mark the beautiful old stone. *Nah that would be just too weird.*

She looks at her reflection in the mirror. She thinks walking and fresh air is helping her complexion. She used very little make-up that morning. She likes the feeling she gets when she is on an adventure. Maybe it's from her sassy new hairstyle.

She shakes her head and... *Who the heck is that?* In the mirror, she can see the top of the swinging door to the stall she just left. There is a little person, a faeire, sitting up there watching her. She is dressed in a sky blue, candy apple red, silver weave body suit. The belt has the same sapphire colored rhinestones that are on the band holding her hair. *Wow, her hair looks like a squashed cotton ball.*

"Hi, are you a London faeire?" Bridget asks, continuing to look in the mirror. She doesn't want to turn around and scare her off. She swallows a laugh as she watches the faeire slip from her perch in shock. She doesn't fly away. She places her right hand to her hair, like an old time cowboy patting his sidearm, straightens her shoulders and flies over to sit on the paper towel dispenser, so she could almost look Bridget in the eye.

'Hi, my name is Bridget."

"I'm Que-tip, but don't get any ideas of zapping me away. I am not as easy a push-over as those in Ireland."

"Oh, you heard about those. Well, I can explain, or at least I think I can."

"Go on then." The feisty little faeire demands.

"They were bespelled fae and the safest place for them were in Cathcart until the war was over and Queen Geraldine could release them."

"You are her then. You are the one the prophecy spoke of, the one that saved us all from Morrigan? I have zillion questions..."

Just then they hear some women coming, "Is there some place private we could go and talk?" Bridget asks.

"Sure, I'll ride along. Your hair is long enough to hide me. Loosen it from that horsetail."

"Sure," Bridget laughs, pulling the rubber band from her hair. "We call it a ponytail, but same idea."

As soon as she has her hair loose, the cute little faeire flies to her shoulder and makes herself comfortable. She covers her with her hair, turns and opens the door. There are three ladies who are laughing and talking in a language Bridget doesn't recognize.

They leave the old stone building that has been remodeled to house the public facilities and Bridget asks, "Which way?"

"You are here to see where the dogs were taken, everyone is. Gawkers we call them. Pay decent money to gawk at other people's troubles. Well, you won't get close you know, it is cordoned off."

Bridget looks over to where another bus load of tourists is heading down the gravel path. "Well, I guess my seeing the crime scene can wait for now. We can go to my car; no one will hear us talking there."

"They can't see me when I shield, at least, no one, except those with a touch of the fae. I thought it would be fun to ride. You must have more than a touch of fae is what I am thinking."

Bridget didn't bother to answer that comment. She didn't know how to. They walk to the parking lot and find her little rental car. She walks to the left-hand side but notices her mistake before she unlocks the door. She can hear a distinct laugh in her ear like the twittering of a bird.

"Okay smarty. This whole steering wheel on the wrong side still messes me up a bit," Bridget admits.

After she unlocks the driver's door and sits behind the steering wheel, she pushes her hair back to allow her guest to fly to the dashboard. She sits Indian style and then just floats up so that Bridget could see her better.

Well, I'm sure, not lonely or bored now. Bridget enjoys watching the little faeire, the expressions on Que-tips very animated face are priceless. She has a pointy little face with high cheekbones, an awesome number of freckles on a shiny pale face, a generous mouth with teeth that have a little gap in the front two and a sharp little nose.

Her tightly curled white hair, held in place by a ring of colorful rhinestones. Que-tip has so much hair it hides her ears; she knows from her other faeire friends in Ireland that her ears are pointed at the top. This faeire is a natural actress, she puts her whole body behind each expression and is a kick to watch.

Que-tip is also staring at Bridget. She sees a pretty girl with the hint of a tan that shows she must have been outdoors. What she sees behind the eyes are what Que-tip likes. She sees that Bridget is a fun, honest person who cares for all living things. She decides there and then they will be friends and says, "You defeated Morrigan, and are alive to tell about it! Wait till I tell the NLFFT's I met you."

"The what?"

"My homies. The Nice Little Fae Folk Tribe."

"Homies, where on earth did you hear that term? That's U.S. slang."

"At the county park," she points with her body to the woods, to the right of the parking lot.

"It has a place for caravans. We gather at night and listen to the young ones. When you meet with us, you will hear a variety of languages."

"When I meet you?"

"Sure, how else are you going to take care of Morrigan evil creatures still out to get revenge without your own army of faeire? We can help; just tell us what we need to do."

"Thanks but I have a wizard and warriors that want to be with me. It is just that I want to be alone. I appreciate the offer to help, but I can handle the evil creatures."

Bridget looks at the faeire and sees how disappointed she is and says, "I do need your help in solving the mystery of where the Dorgis are?"

Que-tip puts her head on her hand and looks deep in thought.

All of a sudden, Bridget is reminded of Mick. She feels sad and wants to be alone. She tells Que-tip, "For now, I'm going to drive to Kings Lynn; I saw an advertisement for hotels, and I want to find a hotel room for the night. That four-hour drive tired me out. What time do the crowds die down around here?"

"Seven P.M. is a fair bet. You want me to meet you then for a private tour?"

"Let's make it much later, how about, Four A.M? I want to make sure I don't get caught trespassing. But I can't park here, where is the best place to meet without my car being noticed?"

Bridget pulls out the map that Michelle had given her. Que-tip flies over the map she has placed against the steering wheel.

"See that spot there?" Que-tip points with her foot. "That is called Stream Walk. You will be coming on the A149 from Kings Lynn. Come up the A149, past the Glucksberg Wood on your right. Take your first right-hand turn. Then take the second right-hand turn past Folly Convert, if you miss it, that's okay, you can take the third right, Folly Hang. They will both bring you past the Wild Wood, and St. Magdalene's Church. Pull off into the Wild Wood, and walk towards Norwich Gates. Find a place to park in among the trees. Walk along that road, and I will be waiting to take you to the Stables Tea Room. The old kennel is just behind there, but it is ready for demolition. They have just been waiting for the go-ahead from MI5. The demolition was scheduled a week ago, now that it is a crime scene, all is on hold."

After those directions, Bridget has a headache. Thank goodness her rental has a GPS. She opens the window to let Que-tip fly off. "I better get going, I'll see you later."

Que-tip doesn't get the hint. She asks, "It won't be light yet, is being able to see in the dark one of your gifts?"

"I wish, but don't worry; I have some things I packed that will help and even dark clothes. They won't spot me. I will see you later."

"I thought you had questions," Que-tip asks with a frown.

"I do, but right now I just need a couple of aspirin and a nap. Bye, see ya later."

Que-tip finally leaves with a flutter of her delicate wings. Bridget hopes she didn't offend her. Speaking with Que-tip reminded her too much of Mick and the Warriors back in Ireland, it made her realize how much she misses them.

She backs the car out, leaves the crowded parking lot and heads south towards, she hopes, the town of Kings Lynn. She holds it together for a few minutes at least until she is on the main road, then the tears come. She pulls over to the side of the road, turns off the engine, and just lets them come.

"I feel a part of a family for the first time in a long time. All I ever wanted was a family who would love me and want me and I have them, but I must leave. I was so happy to have found them. How am I going to leave them?" Bridget cries.

She is so busy sobbing that she doesn't notice a shimmer of light next to her. "What is troubling you dear child?"

"Hi Friar, I'm not very good company right now."

"Perhaps telling me why you are so upset would help." Friar Xavier asks.

"Life is just so unfair! I was so happy!"

"You are not happy now? What has happened?"

Bridget looks embarrassed. "I'm sorry Friar. This is crazy. I have everything. I have no reason not to be happy. Please excuse my tears."

She wipes her eyes and turns to Friar Xavier, wanting to change the subject she says, "I just met a faeire who told me she could help me get into the place where the dogs were last seen. That will help me figure out what happened."

"I think it would be wise to get some assistance. You have a lot on your plate right now helping Michelle, and the Royal family."

"Okay, I guess you're right. Thank you for listening."

"I will be back in touch soon. Take care my child, enjoy your new adventure."

Chapter 9

Kings Lynn Pub
Norfolk, England

The room at Kings Lynn is a little noisy since it is directly over a pub, but it's a beautiful, large, corner room with lots of light provided by its many windows. Bridget did something she never does. But since she told Que-tip she was going to, she lays down for a nap.

Heavy fog shrouds the area. A pale green light glows sickly, barely showing her the way. She feels that she is too cold; She can't go on." Then she hears the voices, *"We are waiting for you. We need you to help us."*

Bridget's leg muscles ache, she is tired. She feels as if she has been walking for hours. She senses someone behind her, turns...

Lucky for Bridget, an Irish bagpiper, begins to play or test his bag. She wakes up first fearful with remnants of the nightmare remaining and then hearing the noise the bagpipes are making, she thinks someone has run over a cat. She jumps out of bed.

According to the ornate clock on the dresser, it is Two A.M. She gets moving to keep her appointment with Que-tip. She showers, and changes into the cat burglar outfit she purchased for her last adventure in Ireland. Best buy she ever made. She puts on a pair of black hiking boots, black jeans, thick black sweater, and a black scarf to cover her hair. Adds a large silver bike chain that she hangs from her front pocket to the back. That way no one would think her outfit strange. She just looks Goth.

Good thing she invested the few extra euros' for her rental's GPS; she could never find her way back at night without it. At the Sandringham grounds, she puts the GPS volume on mute and slows the car to a crawl. She finds the road Que-tip suggested and pulled the car into the trees for extra camouflage. *Hey, I'm getting good*

at this detecting stuff. Just knew watching all of those crime shows would pay off someday.

She quietly closes the car door and using her penlight to guide her, opens the trunk. She pulls out her black backpack, glad she added the extra sweater to the bag to help absorb the noise of the tools banging against each other. When she turns off the light, she looks up at the incredible night sky. Away from the city lights, the stars and constellations look as if you could reach out and touch them. One comes right at her..... "Yikes!"

"Be quiet now, noise travels," Que-tip whispers telepathically.

"You scared me. I thought you were a falling star, and I was about to be bonked on the head."

"I say, mate; you have been bonked already. Move on now. The guards are heading this way."

They hurry across the lawn and keep to the shadows. She forgot to ask if there were dogs on patrol. She learned her lesson in Ireland. If dogs are guarding the property, then she is going home.

"Que-tip, are there any guard dogs I have to worry about?"

"Nah, the Queen's security team is too hi-tech for that. Just bend when I tell you, jump when I tell you, otherwise you will set off the alarms."

They walk for almost an hour. *If Que-tip tells her one more time to bend or jump, she will just scream. Next time the dang backpack stays home, it weighs a ton. She shouldn't complain, this is a good workout.*

"Jump high now!"

Startled, Bridget jumps high but lands wrong. Her feet fly out from under her. She lands on her rump and the backpack. What must have been the rock pick pokes her and she yells, "Ouch."

At the same time, she hears a nearby horse whinny loudly.

"Sorry Que-tip, thanks for the help. What did you do to the poor horse to have him cry to cover up the noise?"

"What would I do to Fred? I just asked him."

"You can talk to animals?"

"You can't?"

"I guess I can." Remembering her animal friends in the Howth Castle woods, and the Red Dragon of Wales, she smiles.

"Hush now, and watch where you are walking. There is the path to the old kennel straight ahead."

Thank goodness for the bright starlit night. Bridget can just make out the kennel. It's an old stone building about the size of a one car garage. She can see where the rock has tumbled loose from the mortar. *No wonder they are tearing it down.* The door is crisscrossed with yellow police tape. *Now to get in,* she ducks beneath the tape, checks out the lock and pulls off her backpack. She carefully removes a plastic card and jimmies the lock.

"How did you learn that?" Que-tip asks.

"From forgetting my key at home when I went to get the mail. A neighbor showed me how to use a card to open my door if only the top lock caught."

"Top lock?"

"We have three locks on our apartment door, a regular lock, a dead bolt and a metal pole that's welded into the door and floor so that no one can just push our door open."

"And you call that a home?"

"It is, or was."

Que-tip tilts her head and says, "Be quick, the guard is coming."

Bridget opens the door as quietly as she can and shuts it just as quietly behind her.

"Que-tip please let me know when it's okay to turn on my flashlight."

"Your what?"

"My torch, I hear critters moving about, and I'd love to turn on a light."

"Okay, the way is clear. He won't be back for another hour."

Bridget turns on her torch and turns to the right. She is looking at a long narrow room with what looks like big wooden toy boxes lined up on one side. She goes over and lifts one of the lids. "What are these?" She asks.

"This is where the staff would feed and water the dogs." Que-tip points down and explains, "You can add the feed and water from here on a rainy day, and the handler will stay dry. Next to the food and water dish is a bed. They are all under shelter here, but if the dogs want, they can run along there (she points to the long dark space beyond the sheltered area) it extends for a dozen meters at least."

Bridget looks at the area Que-tip points out and asks, "If I climb down there could I get out carrying a cage of puppies?"

"Not likely. There are twenty such runs, and each one has a chain link fence separating it from its neighbors. Coming out in broad daylight would draw the attention of the Queen's Guards."

They continue looking around the kennel. Bridget goes back to the front room. It looks like her Aunt Polly's cottage in Ireland. *It might have once been a cottage, and the kennel was added on later.* There is a floor to ceiling stone fireplace that has been taped up to warn people not to get too close. The front room is a good size room. Bridget wonders what it was used for. "This place seems really old. Was it a cottage at one time?" She asks Que-tip.

"When Prince Edward purchased Sandringham for his young bride, he did an extensive remodel. There was a whole section connecting this portion to the old chapel, but that was torn down."

"What was in here most recently?"

Using her whole body to point, Que-tip explains, "There was a big, old, roll-top desk that sat in the corner over there. On the other side of the fireplace there were grooming tables; beyond them were large, deep stainless steel sinks. All of that was taken to the new kennel."

"So it was on one of those tables that Michelle put the cage which held all of the puppies."

"Sure, and Willie helped her to do it. She is weak, couldn't lift the cage by herself. Or as Lynne says, she wanted to flirt with Willie."

"Your friend thought that Michelle wanted to flirt with Willie? Who are Willie and Lynne?"

Que-tip lands on the windowsill and explains, "Willie is a groundsman and Lynne is my best bud. She is a little overprotective of Willie. She thinks all female humans are flirting with him. She likes humans and loves watching them. Willie's eyesight is not as good as it once was, so it is safe for her to hang with him."

"That's great! There is a witness that Michelle placed the cage on the table, and left the building?"

"Don't get your knickers in a twist. We know that Michelle put the cage on the table and that Willie left right away. No one saw the dogs after that. They just disappeared."

They continue to look around for another half-hour, but they can't see anything of any use.

How did she ever think that she could accomplish what others could not? She is getting ready to leave when she stops to admire the large old stone fireplace. "How old do you think this building is?" Bridget asks.

"I would say it is not too old at all, several hundred years or so."

Bridget smiles at Que-tip's view of 'not too old'; she keeps forgetting that the fae think in centuries rather than years. "Since this was part of a much larger 'keep' they might have had a chapel on the property and a priest available for the family. Perhaps this cottage was for the priest."

"Then it must have been before my birth." Que-tip tilts her head to the side and says, "Bridget, we had better leave now, I hear someone coming."

"You're right," she whispers though she doesn't hear anyone. "Maybe I could return another time, and look some more."

"Possibly!"

"What do you mean, possibly?"

"It is scheduled to be torn down."

"Let me do some more research on-line tonight and we can try again tomorrow."

Then she hears the sound of strong, determined steps on the gravel driveway out front.

"Hurry, hide," she whispers, as she moves the tape, and takes cover in the extra-large hearth of the old fireplace. Que-tip flies to her shoulder.

The guard opens the door. He carries a torch that lights up the entire room. As he swings the light around the dark room, he shouts "Who goes there, show yourself now."

Bridget knows he will soon discover their hiding place. She presses back farther into the hearth and feels the cold stones at her back. Bridget stretches out her right hand and leans against the back wall to get her balance. The entire back opens; they fall through into complete darkness.

A few of the old bricks fall, and she hears the guard speak into his cell. "The old bricks are falling. Must be what I heard, all clear here."

She feels a slight breeze on her face and hears a whispered question from Que-tip, "Where the bloody heck are we?"

The hearth opening swings closed behind them. They are in complete darkness. The dust, mold, and damp go to work on her eyes and nose right away. She begins to sneeze. She covers her mouth and squeezes her nose. The sound that escapes is a little strange. It sounds like a very loud squeal.

She hears the guard say to himself "No one is here, just my imagination." He hurries from the room that makes strange sounds with no one to be seen.

"Que-tip, could you please help me find my torch, I lost it when we fell into this secret room."

"Secret room?"

"Sure, don't teen faeire read the history of their country? This room must be a major clue. I bet it's a priest hole; perhaps this cottage was once a part of a chapel. During the Reformation, the English priest would grab any signs that he was holding mass and hide. If he were captured, he would be imprisoned or killed. Let's check it out."

Bridget finds her flashlight and turns it on. The light illuminates a galvanized steel crate with bars. The door of the crate is open; she starts to shiver. She walks over to the crate and touches the bars. The images of her nightmare return. She can see the puppies and the gloved hand.

"Bridget, what is happening? Why are you crying?" An anxious Que-tip asks.

Bridget takes a few deep breaths to shake off the images and is finally able to answer, "I saw the puppies. We have to find the guy who did this, we must."

"So you are psychometric? Like you have the ability to sense things by touch?"

"I don't think so, maybe? In this case, I saw what was happening in a nightmare the other day. I just recalled it now. Let's take a look around and see if we can spot anything that they may have left behind. Hopefully, something that would give us a clue as to who they are."

Stone totally encloses the small room; she has to shake the feeling that she is buried alive. She feels sorry for any priest that had to hide in there for any length of time. Crawling around is difficult. There is a lot of rubble on the floor, but she can't make out what kind of rubble it is. Then they both spot it at the same time, a glove.

"What is that?" Que-tip asks.

Bridget reaches into her pocket for a tissue and uses it to pick up the large, black faux leather glove. She has a large zip-lock bag that she knew would come in handy as an evidence bag. As she places the glove into the bag, there is a loud rumble.

"What's that noise?" A frightened Que-tip asks.

"Sounds like a massive piece of machinery to me, let's get out of here." She tucks the bag inside her jacket and turns back to the wall that had opened to let them enter. The large stone wall had shut behind them automatically. "There has to be a way to open it from this side."

They push and prod every stone on that wall for what seems like hours, and then the flashlight battery gives out.

"I learned the Scouts have it right, always be prepared." She reaches into her backpack for a new package of batteries and begins to tear it open. "Now why do they have to make everything child proof, I can't get these dang things open." Bridget is sitting on the ground Indian style, struggling with the package of batteries, the noise is getting louder.

"You are magic, do something!" cries Que-tip.

"What do you mean, do something? I can't do anything. Heck, I can't even get this dang package open."

"But you are of Royal Blood; you must be able to do magic."

A nervous Bridget answers as more rock and rubble fall around them. "Okay, I learned to be grateful for what I have, learned to be positive. Learned how to banish evil faeire, accept all living creatures and stop worrying about the future, to fly, to move to where I want to be. But I'm not sure of getting through walls."

"You must be able to do something. The old scrolls tell us that you have freed all fae kind."

"I know who can do magic, Mick!" She shouts, "I need you, Mick. Mick, please come as fast as possible. We're in danger! Help!"

They feel the ground rumble and hear more stones falling around them.

Chapter 10

**Sandringham Castle
Norfolk, England**

"What is this you are telling me? How on earth did you get into so much trouble in just two days? I spoke with you every day," asks a not too happy Mick.

"Well, you asked if I was doing okay and I am, well, sort of. You asked whenever you called ..."

Mick stood bent over, looking down at where Bridget was sitting on the floor still trying to open the batteries. Before he can yell some more she continues explaining. "When you asked if I saw the sights, I told you I did. When you asked, where I had been, I told you: Buckingham Palace, St. Paul's Cathedral, the family home of the Queen and..."

"True." Mick interrupts, "Somehow, you neglected to tell me that the reason you were in St. Paul's Cathedral was that you found your English cousin. Who happens to believe that you are destined to join him in stopping its destruction?"

"Well, it's not like I have done anything about that yet."

"But you plan to?" shrieks Mick.

"Hey, don't shriek at my friend," demands Que-tip.

Ignoring her, Mick continues, "You also neglected to mention, this young lady here, a teenage hoodlum if ever I saw one."

"Hey watch it, buddy, I may be small, but I have friends in high places."

Que-tip flies a few inches above Mick's eyes. Her little body is shaking as she confronts a wizard a hundred times her size. She is pointing her finger at him, and the large head of white, cotton ball looking hair, is shaking from side to side.

"Oh, pardon me, Miss Ear Wax is it? How did you talk Bridget into this scheme that has her locked in an ancient priest hole? A priest hole that is about to be knocked down by a bloody wrecking ball."

"Mick, I never said she talked me into it if you would only listen. Practice what you have been teaching me, okay? Take a deep breath. Que-tip is a teenage faeire, which of course, is why she can hear you speak.

She is going to help me find the Queen's dogs. But before she does, she wants me to come and speak with her group."

"Help you do what?"

"I shouldn't be speaking with you about all of this now, but I do need your help in getting out of here, and like soon please. I can hear that wrecking ball. It's getting closer."

Bridget could see that Mick is ready to argue some more, he so likes to argue with her, so she interrupts before he gets going again.

"It was Friar Xavier who got me here. Well, he and Michelle. Except Michelle cannot see the Friar since he's the ghost who watches over the Royal Family." She hears a low growl and talks a little faster.

"Well, you see the Queen raises Corgi's, and she has bred them with Dachshunds. Now she is the proud owner of a new breed called Dorgis. Except someone has dognapped the puppies! Michelle was caring for them, and she is from France.

"The papers are blaming the French people. It's not right! It's a mess. So I'm just investigating. Que-tip and I discovered this place, and we got locked in."

The sound of large machinery is almost on top of them. Large pieces of rock begin to follow the dirt and small chunks of mortar that has been coming down.

"Mick, can you get us out......like now!" Bridget shouts.

Mick closes his eyes. *How can I ever let her out of my sight? When she is not close, it is as if a part of me is missing. The thought of her being hurt is too much to bear.* He nods his head and flicks his hand.

Bridget closes her eyes and covers her face to stop inhaling the dust. She feels like she is back in the wind tunnel ride at Coney Island. Her feet no longer touch the ground. She feels like she is in a blender being tossed around. She uncovers her eyes but can't see anything except a dense fog with what looks like Christmas lights flickering. Finally, it stops, and she can feel grass under her. She looks around and realizes that she is lying next to her rental car.

"Que-tip, where are you? Are you okay?"

"What a trip, thank you... Ah, Mick was it?"

"Nothing you couldn't have done yourself." Mick snaps.

Bridget looks at Que-tip, "What does he mean; could you have gotten us out of there?"

"I could have left anytime. But what type of a friend would I be if I left you behind?"

Mick scowls at Bridget, "Why didn't you use the transporter spell?" When she looks puzzled, he explains, "When I taught you to get yourself down from the tree in Ireland, I told you just to concentrate on where you want to be, and it will happen."

"I didn't know it would work when I was enclosed in solid rock." An embarrassed Bridget explains.

"Thank you Que-tip, and thank you, Mick. Whew that was a trip, now I have to get to Scotland Yard and give them the evidence we found."

"Why not turn it over to the constable here?"

"Que-tip, if I go to someone local then they may arrest me for breaking in on a crime scene.

"You are taking it to the Yard for an opportunity to visit with the inspector you met at Heathrow when you came over?"

"Mick, don't sound so grumpy, and what I told a dog should stay with the dog. Charlie is a smart cop, and he knows me. Besides, what's wrong with using this as an opportunity to meet up with Charlie again? He did say he would show me around London if I ever made the trip over here."

"So who is Charlie?" Que-tip asks.

"As Mick says I met him when he worked at Heathrow. He sent me a note telling me that he is now a detective inspector assigned to the Criminal Investigation Department or the CID. His office is in the New Scotland Yard. I have his card. I'll call him, and hopefully, he can see us right away."

They all pile into the car for the trip to London. Que-tip is looking in the rearview mirror and dusting herself off. "Bridget, I think you may wish to stop at your room at the Inn for a quick dust off."

Bridget looks down at her black outfit that is now white with dust. "You think?"

♣♣♣

They luck out and find a parking place right in front of the Hard Rock Café. It's not a quiet out of the way place, but it was Que-tip's choice. She looked so excited at getting a chance to go to a place she had heard about, that Bridget figured Charlie could put up with a little noise.

Mick decided he's needed in Ireland and with a shimmer and scowl at Que-tip and a reminder to stay safe, he was gone.

Bridget timed the meeting just right. There are no lines in front of the restaurant, but she notices the gift shop next door is packed. When she opens the large impressive door, they are hit with sound. Elvis is singing Jailhouse Rock, and there are more than a hundred people from various cultures all talking at once.

She wishes she could see the look on Que-tip's face as she takes in the décor. She can feel her excitement from the flutter of her wings against her neck.

"I have to get a closer look," Que-tip informs her as she flies up towards the ceiling. When Bridget sees where she is headed, she laughs out loud; there are

guitars, drums and all sorts of things up there to amuse her. She is sure Que-tip will enjoy herself.

Charlie comes over; he looks up to see what Bridget is laughing at and sees the old time memorabilia on the ceiling and smiles and says, "It's a fun place. Let's get a seat."

A waitress in a poodle skirt straight from the fifties shows them to a booth in the back. It is a little quieter. The menu is good, and they both order cheeseburgers. While they wait for the food, they both look around at all of the great signed photographs, records, costumes, and instruments. When the food arrives, Bridget realizes that she is starving. *It must be all of the excitement.*

She is halfway done with her burger when Charlie says, "Bridget it is grand to see you again. You mentioned you had some evidence to give me."

She knows he's laughing at her and thinks her "evidence" was just an excuse to see him again. Charlie has the dreamiest eyes but too big of an ego. She reluctantly puts down her burger and reaches into her handbag for the glove securely sealed in the zip-lock plastic bag. She explains about meeting Michelle, leaving out Friar Xavier of course, her visit to the old kennel, finding the priest hole and barely getting out in time.

"You entered a building that had been posted?"

Charlie's eyes were no longer dreamy; they show his anger and concern for her safety. Heck, she thought meeting in a fun restaurant would soften this lecture part of the conversation. To get him focused on problem-solving, she suggests, "You can still recover the crate and perhaps dust that for fingerprints. It may be a little squished but it was a high-quality steel crate, it should still be recognizable."

He takes out his cell and asks to be connected to the Sandringham Garda. As she listens to his side of the conversation, she finishes her burger.

He completes his call, reaches into his pocket and throws twenty euros on the table. "I have no idea how I am going to explain all of this without bringing you into it, but I will try. Are you staying at the flat in Battersea?"

"Yes. Will you let me know as soon as you find out anything?"

"Okay, but you must promise to leave the detecting to CID. You are a tourist, see the sights."

"I have, really I can't get into any trouble. There is no more that I can think of to do to find the puppies. It's all in your hands now. I'm going to meet my cousin tonight and have a nice family dinner."

He looks her over with a piercing look that she often gets from Mick. "I had better get to it. I will call you in a few days." Charlie gets up and walks to the front door as Que-tip flies down to her shoulder.

"He did not look very pleased that we solved his case for him."

"He hasn't caught them yet, but he will. Want to have something to eat?"

Que-tip looks at the scrapes of Bridget's burger and shutters. "No thank you, but I would like to have a Coke."

Bridget places a to-go order with the waitress for a milkshake she could share with Que-tip. No Coke for her, that's all she needs, a crazed faeire on a caffeine high. They head back to the flat for a well-deserved nap.

Chapter11

**Workman's Pub
Battersea, England**

Bridget wakes up with a start and jumps out of bed. She just knows she is late for work and rushes to the bathroom. She trips over a chair and finally wakes up enough to realize it's the phone ringing and not the alarm clock. Looking around the bedroom, she remembers where she is. *It isn't dark outside; I haven't slept very long.*

"Hello."

"Is this Bridget?"

"Yes, who's calling?"

"This is your cousin Peter."

"Hi, how are you doing?"

"I am grand, thank you. I wish to speak with you. Do you have time to meet up?"

"I would love to meet you. Would you like to come to Battersea? I could make us some dinner."

"That would be grand. What time would work for you?"

She quickly glances at her cell to check the time. It's only two p.m. She only slept for an hour, no wonder she feels horrible. Thinking quickly, she would have to go grocery shopping, take another shower to wake up, cook. *Ah, the heck with it.* "Why don't we meet somewhere, it might be easier."

"There is a pub called the Workman's on High Street, do you know of it? It has great sharers."

"Sharers?"

"Yes, they are appetizers. I went to a party there, and it's a good spot. Would that be acceptable, or would you prefer another place?"

"No, that will be fine. I have a GPS; I'll find it. Will parking be a problem?"

"Shouldn't be if we get there early. Say five p.m., would that work for you?"

Bridget knows Peter is anxious to meet with her and bring her up to date on his search for the abandoned underground tunnel. *I wish I knew how I could help. Hopefully, I'll think of something.*

"That'll be great. I'll see you there."

As he says goodbye and hangs up the phone, Bridget realizes she has no idea what to wear. She will go for dressy casual; a girl can never go wrong with classy. She gathers up her robe and heads for the shower. Maybe she will think clearer after a hot shower.

She bumps into an excited Que-tip. "I am glad you are going to meet him at a pub. I loved the Hard Rock Café. Will this one be as grand?"

With a flash, Lord Howth appears in human form. "If everyone is going then I am too," he states.

"Oh no, you don't Mick, you can stay here and rest, or better yet, you can go home. I don't want to explain a man in my room or one that just likes to hang out with me. I'll be fine. This is just a meeting with my cousin. No big deal." She hurries into the shower over their protests.

"Mick you cannot come in with me. I'm not going to make believe that I'm blind so that you would be welcomed as a seeing eye dog. You insisted on coming. I don't care if you shape-shifted into a Brittany spaniel. You have two choices; you can go home, or you will have to wait in the car."

"Ms. Ear Wax gets to come with you."

Bridget can't believe a wizard over a hundred years old sounds like a spoiled brat. She shakes her head. Before Que-tip could start in on Mick, she opens the car door and looks back at Mick. "The only reason I let you come in the first place is that you promised to remain in dog form when humans are around. I haven't explained everything to my cousin yet. I need to know him longer before I can do that."

She hears him mumble and knowing that he is only here because he is concerned for her, she quietly says, "You can leave at any time. Please don't worry about me, Mick. I will be okay, honest."

Mick looks at her with a very clear doggie scowl.

"Okay, have it your way. I don't need a babysitter, but if you insist," She gives him a devilish smile and says, "I've left all of the windows down in case you want to use a tree, but please don't leave the car unless you really need to. I would hate to have a rental stolen."

She hears Mick say something, as she quickly walks away.

"What does your cousin look like?" an excited Que-tip asks as Bridget opens a large oak door with a stained glass insert.

"A lot like my dad. I hope the place isn't crowded."

As soon as her eyes adjust to the dark interior, she spots him. She gasps and hears from both Mick and Que-tip.

"What is wrong...?"

"I am coming in...."

"No, please you two, everything's okay. It's just a flashback. My dad died when I was young, but I still think of him a lot."

Peter is leaning against a bar stool with his back to the bar, intently watching the front door. Bridget is flooded with emotions. She walks towards Peter, and he meets her halfway.

"Hi Bridget, I forgot to tell you that you are the spitting image of your Aunt Winnie, did you know that, gave me a start for a moment."

She manages to say, "You are the spitting image of my dad."

"Let's have a seat at one of the booths in the back. We have a great deal to talk about."

A waitress comes over, and they order a "sharer" and tea.

"How have you been amusing yourself?" Peter asks.

She tells him of her drive to Norfolk and her stay at Kings Lynn and that she has fallen in love with the English countryside. She notices the sadness in his eyes and asks, "Is everything okay?"

"I was locating a missing child. I felt I should have been working on St. Paul's but I could not say no to the mom."

"Before I left for Norfolk, I visited St. Paul's Cathedral. I saw a chapel dedicated to the American Soldier. It's beautiful. There was also a painting there that gave me the shivers."

"I know the one you are referring to; I get the same reaction. St. Paul's Cathedral became an inspiration to the British people during the Second World War. It miraculously escaped major bomb damage while buildings in the surrounding areas were reduced to rubble. Do you know that a total of 28 bombs landed on St. Paul's during the Blitz? It only survived because of the volunteers that made up the St. Paul's Watch. Images of St. Paul's framed by the smoke and fire caused by the bombing became a symbol of our nation's indomitable spirit."

Bridget leans forward and says, "So if you want to hurt the people of England, what better way than to destroy someplace that means so much?"

"Exactly."

"I don't understand. What brings people to want to destroy such a wonderful, historic building? It just doesn't make sense to me." She looks down at the plate of hummus, pita bread and veggies the waitress delivered, suddenly not very hungry.

"The way I see it, they must hate what the church stands for. People teach their kids to hate; it is not something we are born with. I had a teacher once who helped to open my eyes. Her lecture that day was entitled 'Believe in something, or fall for anything.'"

"That makes sense to me; it is something my mom would say."

"She asked us to fold a sheet of paper in three columns. On the first column, she had us write important subject headers, such as religion, wealth, environment, etc. On the second column, we were asked to write what we believed on the subject. We were asked not to think about it, just write down our beliefs. No one would see this paper; it was just for our benefit. On the third column, we were asked to look at all of the answers we wrote in column two and then think about when we first heard that comment, thought, whatever.

"I realized then that I had few thoughts of my own; they were mostly from my parents, friends, neighbors, or the newspapers. For example with the topic of global warming, I wrote 'another way the government wants to take our money.' Can you believe it? Where did that come from? When I thought about it, it was a loud, cranky neighbor, whom no one liked, but he was well read, and we listened to his opinion and believed him. It was easier to take on someone else's belief than do the research to find out the facts.

"After that class, I found myself in the library checking out the stories on global warming, the war in the middle east, the Holocaust, and heck even the crusades so I might begin to under- stand how and why some of the wars over religious differences started. I studied just about everything I had an opinion on. I wanted it to be my opinion, not someone else's. Hey, I even got angry that I allowed others to tell me how to believe without checking out the facts for myself.

"The people who want to blow up St. Paul's never had a teacher who asked them to stop and think why they believe what they do. They don't know if it is a cranky neighbor. They are just taught to hate and go blindly into that hate. If someone is a different color, different size or a different race or a different religion, why would you use your energy to hate them? I could see not liking a person who did you wrong, but a whole race or group of people? It just does not make sense to me."

Bridget nods her head. "I agree it doesn't make sense to me either."

"Sorry for sounding like I am on a soapbox. That teacher made a difference in my life. The class discussed their thoughts on the subject of beliefs later, and several of the foreign students got misty eyed when they realized what the word freedom means. We are free to believe what we want, not what others tell us to believe. That little exercise impacted all of us big time."

"That's awesome, what a great teacher."

"She was."

Peter lifts his cup to take a long drink, and Bridget notices that he is showing the strain he's under. The other night she thought he was just tired from his trip. He has dark circles under his eyes and a haunted look. She thinks his nightmares are frequent and are really bad. He's young, maybe twenty-four, but he looks tired and worn out. *Are these 'gifts' worth it?* She enjoys helping others as Peter said he did, but at what price?

Bridget looks up, and Que-tip has finished her investigation of the sports channel and is sprinkling dust and blowing it at Peter. For a moment, she was going to ask her what she was doing but thought she would wait and see. At first, nothing happened. Then out of nowhere a lively breeze whirled around them, a breeze that feels full of hope and humor. Que-tip tugs at her top straighten her shoulders and pats her hairdo as if she just gave herself a pat on the back for a job well done. She looks at Bridget and winks.

Peter looks at her and smiles. He looks so much better. It's as though he has some of his strength and confidence back. "Bridget you have a beautiful smile. What has you in such a fine humor?"

"Just thinking of some folks I met in Ireland. I can't wait for you to meet them. I'm taking a break from training. When I learn all of the gifts I have been given, I will be able to do many things. It's still very hard to wrap my mind around."

"I can understand that feeling, and I only have the one gift. I do have to admit that there is no better feeling in the world than the one you get when you know you have helped someone in need."

"Speaking of need, how are you doing with St. Paul's, any leads?"

"No luck on a map but one bloke told me to go to the British Legion. It is located not far from St. Paul's. There are fellows who grew up in that neighborhood. Some had dads who were part of the St. Paul's watch during the war. They may know much more than anyone else does."

"Sounds like a plan, when do we go?"

"As soon as we finish eating, okay to take your car? I came over by tube."

"Sure, you'll just have to put up with Mick."

"Mick?"

"He is a dog and a very good friend. It seems I can't go anywhere without him." She smiles and begins eating.

"No problem."

Chapter 12

British Legion
Battersea, England

They locate a parking place on a side road. Brick townhouses and colorful flowering gardens, surrounded by wrought iron fencing line the street. Not a high-class neighborhood, but one that shows the people care. It's well maintained with no graffiti and no gates on the doors or windows. This is another community where the neighbors watch out for one another.

The building where the British Legion is located is very different from the American Legion buildings Bridget has seen. This is not a plain square building in the center of a parking lot. The British Legion is located on the ground floor of a brownstone, three story walk-up. It looks as if it is part of the neighborhood. You enter from street level. The design is slightly different from its neighbors. No steps are leading up to the second floor from the street, so all stairs must be on the inside.

They walk into a long narrow room. On the left, next to the door is a small stage. A tall, distinguished, older woman with jet black hair is singing and playing the piano. The furniture looks like what you would expect to find in a pub. Beautiful old wood, leather chairs and tables. Some tables against the wall are set to seat two or four. A few toward the back are joined to seat six to a dozen patrons at a time. At the back of the room is a small bar. Over the bar is a large mirror. *Now that's clever. The mirror shows the bartender who's coming in, even when he has his back to the door.*

Peter pulls out a chair at the table for twelve, "Have a seat here a second and I will speak with the barkeep."

A few minutes' later men who look like they are in their eighties come over to sit with Bridget. She smiles but doesn't know what to say. Peter comes back with a couple of pitchers of beer, and she notices the guys come over with glasses in hand.

"Drink up lads; my cousin here wants to thank you for the grand chapel that is dedicated to the American soldier. There is plenty more where this came from, enjoy."

Peter set a glass with dark liquor topped with foam in front of her. She hopes it isn't Guinness. She tried a sip in Ireland, and a sip was enough. She picks it up and sniffs, thankfully its root beer. After a few dozen comments of, "Brilliant," "Welcome Miss," she begins to talk about St. Paul's, the chapel and the painting of St. Paul's during the Blitz.

Six men sit with them and a few shuffle back to the bar. The men tell them stories of families who survived and the losses they endured, the rebuilding of a city. It is all incredible; she could have stayed and listened to them for hours. Then Peter asks, "Was there a bomb shelter around that you used when Gerry was coming?"

All are silent, deep in thought. One fellow with a mass of white hair that helps to highlight his sky blue eyes removes his pipe and calls out, "Hey Maggie, me girl, come over, join us for a pint, a gift from the good lady here."

Bridget turns to see who George is speaking with and notices a dark shadow rise from a seat against the wall. She'd been hidden from view by the stage. There is only room for one chair and no table where she was sitting. Bridget has a strong feeling that Maggie is a woman who prefers her own company but likes the noise of people around.

It's very warm in the Legion Hall, but Maggie is wearing a heavy black wool coat with a large, faded, red, silk flower. Her bright orange wig is held on with a bright green satin ribbon covered with more silk flowers. She walks very slowly and sits in a chair behind George.

"Please join us, Maggie, would you like something to drink?"

Maggie shakes her head as she seemed to duck behind George, as if for protection. *Wow, I wonder what her life was like, what stories she could tell.*

George repeats Peter's question to Maggie, but Bridget can't hear what her answer is.

George turns to Peter, "Maggie and her family took cover in the Underground at Foster Lane. It ain't there now, been shut up tight for years."

"Why would they close a tube station in this area, don't they need all they can use?" Bridget asks.

"As if one can understand anything the government does these days." George finished off his beer and held up his empty glass for a refill. He shakes his head and says, "Who knows, it could be ready to fall in?"

All the British Legionnaires pipe in then with one of the major entertainments in any bar, sharing opinions, no matter how crazy. Bridget and Peter hear everything from the old tube station being unsafe, being haunted, to government cutbacks. After they get the directions to Foster Lane, they start to leave. Peter announces that the tab is still open for anyone to enjoy a pint or two on the American. They leave the building, and Bridget is glad to breathe fresh air. She is happy that most public places have a no smoking ban. There was a lot of smoke in one small place.

"Okay if we walk to Foster Lane, Mick could use a walk."

Bridget goes over to the car and is happy to see that Mick is still there. Mick smells her clothes and sneezes. "It is cigarette smoke." Mick looks up at her, *"Don't worry; I'm too smart to smoke."*

"Sure, it isn't far from here." Peter's smartphone shows a map of the area that includes all the current underground stations and bus routes.

"Bridget, could you take a look at this, and tell me what you make of it?" he asks. "Do you see anything unusual?"

"I see Foster Lane, but the current neighborhood station is almost a mile away from here at Newgate Street. Why make everyone walk that far when Foster Lane is so much closer. That doesn't make sense to me."

"Keep looking!" Peter says as he uses a stylus to click on the arrows to move the screen in an easterly direction.

"Oh no! If there's a deserted tunnel, it may go underneath not only St. Paul's, but Fleet Street, and the Exchange. They are right near one another. They may be planning to take down all three!"

"That would also give us a reason why it has been abandoned. A tunnel directly under the Exchange would be a threat to the country's economic structure." Peter explains.

"Let's find it!" Bridget turns and says, "Mick and Que-tip, we need your help with this; the opening has been shut down a long time. No telling where it is."

"Who is Que-tip?" Asks Peter.

Dang, I forgot to speak telepathically. "It's okay Peter; I will explain in a minute."

"Que-tip, stay with Bridget, I can sniff it out." says Mick.

Que-tip flies to her spot on Bridget's shoulder, as she releases Mick from his leash.

"You just want an excuse to run after being stuck in the car. Whatever you do, please don't get picked up by the dog catcher, you still don't have a license," Bridget giggles.

She hears a growl, and a laugh from Peter as Mick swiftly disappears around the corner.

"Mick doesn't look happy, was that growling a way of communicating with you?" an amused Peter asks.

"Yes, he does that often when I hurt his doggie pride. He's a character, but he'll help us find the station now that we have some idea where to look."

They walk about ten blocks. Bridget takes this opportunity to tell Peter about their relatives in Ireland, the fae war, and that Mick, her teacher, is actually Lord Howth and was made to take the form of a dog by order of the Fae Queen. And that he continues to appear as a dog since it is easier to explain a dog hanging around her all the time then it would be if he was in human form.

"Even when he is in human form I call him Mick. He doesn't like it much, but I think he is getting used to it."

She also tells Peter how she met her new friend, a faeire called Que-tip. During her long explanation, Peter stops, in shock, his mouth opens but no words come out.

"I know it is a little overwhelming but you sort of get used to the magic of it all." she takes Peter's arm to move him along.

When Peter finally finds the words, all he can say is, "That dog is an English Lord?" He shakes his head. "This is a bit overwhelming, but I sensed you had a great deal of talent. It is hard to believe this all happened only six months ago. You must be ready for a vacation. I'm sorry I dragged you into this mess."

"That is what family is for. To help one another when in need, right?" Bridget smiles and continues to hold his arm.

They turn a corner to a much older section of storefronts and dirty alleys. They walk past a grocer with an old faded awning, under which are large wooden boxes filled with fruit that has seen better days. Most of the fruit is spotted, and the flies have gathered.

Bridget smells the aroma of fresh bread. They follow the smell and her phone's GPS and find a baker half way down an alley. The Baker has no storefront, but there are large vents blowing smoke up into the air.

Peter suggests, "That baker must sell to the larger stores, and use this warehouse for a base."

They look around for a possible Underground entrance. The alley goes behind many small apartment buildings. The backyards are typical of those she would see in New York. Clothes-lines hang from windows to poles that are strung with blankets, and sheets hung to dry. In one of the many buildings, someone is playing a high whining instrument, the sights and sounds remind Bridget of Brooklyn.

Not seeing any possible entrance, they are about to turn around and leave the alley when Bridget hears Mick, *"Come to the end of the alley. You will see a large wooden door. It looks like it leads to another warehouse, but as soon as you get inside, you will see the entrance to the tube."*

Bridget tells Peter what Mick has found. They rush to the end of the alley to join him. It is starting to get dark. She is happy that Peter remembered to bring a flashlight.

Somehow Mick opened a very large lock and removed the chain that had been wrapped around a metal pole. It is so rusted it must not have been opened for years.

Peter looks at the lock and winks at Bridget, "Pretty impressive for a dog."

They are both quiet as they tiptoe into the old station. Peter takes the lead, which is fine with Bridget since he gets to knock down most of the cobwebs.

To keep her mind off any possible creepy crawlies, Bridget looks around at the entrance that appears to be a much smaller size than the larger tube stations she has seen, like Paddington.

They are walking on a floor of beautiful old tile, about the size of nickels, and cut octagonal. If cleaned they would be a bright yellow color with black grout. The walls have the standard large white subway tile, but the name of the station is designed in a repeat of the floor tile.

Peter sweeps the station with his light. Bridget can make out ticket booths that are shrouded in cobwebs and many years of dust that the faint breeze from the open door is stirring around.

"This does not make sense. It looks as if we are the first people to come in here in a long time. But in my vision, I have seen three men and a railroad track, and this feels like the correct location. Could there be another entrance?" Peter asks.

"Might be if you think your vision is happening now and not in the future. You are right; we are the first to come into this entrance in quite a while. See how thick the dust is and no footprints."

A worried looking Peter says, "It might be in the future; I wish I knew for certain. Let's keep looking, I am going down to the platform, do you want to stay here? Those stairs may not be safe."

"Hey, you have the only light; I'm going with you."

"*Bridget?*"

"Don't worry Mick; I'll be okay, where are you?"

"*Peter, can you hear me?*"

"Yes, I can. Imagine that. That is brilliant."

Bridget can hear the awe in Peter's voice. Being an old hat at magic, a talking dog didn't seem to faze him too much.

"*Both of you hug the wall on the way down. The railing is too frail to hold for much longer.*"

Peter's light is no help at all. She can see in front of him but not in front of where she is stepping. She is slowly stepping down one step at a time, trying not to touch the old wall that gives off a horrible smell of mold and mildew. Peter stops. The light reaches out faint fingers of light all around. She can make out the walls that contain shreds of old advertisements, half torn away and faded with time. One reads, 'Careless Talk Costs Lives,' telling them when the station was closed.

"Look at the posters! Maybe it was hit by a bomb during the war."

"Stay here; I'll check the track," Peter advises.

"Wait I'll... Bridget feels herself falling and holds onto the wall.

Blackness and silence, no not complete silence, I can hear my breath and feel my heart race.

Someone else is here...; he's making scraping sounds as he moves.

Blackness. He's carrying a light in his left hand and in its glow I can see him gazing back at me. He's tall and wearing an exotic outfit. It looks like a black tuxedo with embroidered flowers. His face? It looks familiar. He has heavy black eyebrows that are not completely covered by the thick, black-rimmed glasses. He smiles, and I almost return his smile until I notice that in his right hand he is holding a large black gun pointed directly at me.

My feet are frozen in place; I open my mouth to yell for Mick, but no sound comes. I know I can save myself, but I can't think. A flash of light, a muffled pop, I look down at my chest, where there had once been a clean, crisp white shirt, there is blood...a lot of blood.

"Bridget, are you okay?"

"I'm..." Bridget presses her hand against her chest, no blood. What the heck? She moves her hand to the wall to help her to sit up and her blood freezes. *I can feel it all at once, the pain, the fear of dying, the horrible loss of those killed. What gives, now I am seeing and feeling the past, and perhaps ...even my future?*

With a forceful nudge of his head, Mick pushes her hand away from the wall.

Bridget sits back down, "Thank you, Mick."

Mick takes human form and says, "Thank Que-tip there; she is the one who told me you *now* have the gift of Psychometry."

A worried looking Peter stares at the impressive human form of Lord Michael Howth. *This gent is the little dog, well I'll be?* Recovering his shock, he asks, "What is Psychometry?"

Bridget looks over at Peter and understanding he is a bit overwhelmed with everything, she quietly explains, "It's a form of extra-sensory perception. Mick has taught me that most objects have an energy field that transfers knowledge regarding that object's history."

"That's brilliant!"

"Can be, once I learn to control it, right now I have to be careful touching things that may give off negative imprints."

"Would have been nice to know that your gifts are increasing," Mick grumbles.

"Yea, I meant to mention that."

Que-tip flies over from her close up view of the posters. "What happened? Are you okay?"

I feel like I blacked out. Was I pushed down the stairs? But there's no one else here. Mick or Que-tip would have sensed them, wouldn't they?

"Just missed my step and fell, must have knocked my head on the wall. Was I out for long?"

"Out?" Mick asks.

"You know, passed out. I had the strangest dream."

"Bridget, you were just dazed for a second."

She looks at the worried faces around her, "Sorry about that. Must be the history I was picking up from the wall. Let's get onto the track and see where it leads."

Peter reaches out, and she grasps his hand for help in getting up. She gets up too quickly and feels dizzy. She takes one step and yells, "Darn, I think I sprained my ankle."

"You need that iced and bandaged right away. You all stay here. I will get the car." Peter calls out as he turns to leave.

Bridget knows he feels guilty that she got hurt, and calls out, "Peter, I'm okay, don't worry."

"I am not worried, didn't you ever hear that we English are cool and under control at all times?"

"Sure, but don't you think you may need the car keys?"

"Ah. Right, you are. Here keep the torch, I will be okay. Mick, see that she stays put."

Bridget looks at Que-tip and grumbles, "Men are all the same aren't they?"

"You can say that again." Que-tip agrees.

"What do you two mean by that?" A puzzled Lord Howth asks.

"Rather than admit he is upset or worried about her, Peter got bossy and rushed to do something away from here," Que-tip explains.

Bridget looks over at Mick and continues to explain. "I think all that he has learned about magic has ruffled him a bit. He didn't even give me a chance to explain that you can transport me back to Battersea. A woman would handle the situation a little differently. If he were hurt, I would first make sure he was comfortable, maybe assist him to street level rather than leave him here in the dark and dirt."

"But he left you the torch?" Lord Howth looks puzzled.

Que-tip and Bridget look at each other and smile. He just shakes his head. Bridget leans against the post, refusing to sit on the floor again. She gently flexes her leg, testing to see if pain shouts the news of broken bones or torn muscles. No major pain, it is bruised, but aside from the throb, it seems okay. She notices the dirt on her outfit.

"I must look a mess, best that he gets the car. I don't want to walk ten blocks looking like this."

"You could transport yourself you realize, or I could get you home. Why are you waiting for your cousin?" Lord Howth asks.

"He needs something to do right now. Seeing you in human form is a bit overwhelming to us mere mortals. Why don't you two continue inspecting the tunnel?" Bridget asks knowing she needs time to think about what just happened. *Okay, it's not the wall that brought the vision of my race through the tunnel. I've seen that guy before, but where? Was the vision showing me I was going to be shot? What the heck was that? Was that me? That had better not be a sign of what is to come.*

"Hey guys, I think we need more help on this," Bridget calls out.

"Who, we can't go to the Inspector at Scotland Yard, he will not believe this 'intuition' of Peter's."

"You're right the normal avenue is closed for now. Que-tip, could you get a message to Friar Xavier?"

"Sure."

"Please show him where I live and ask him to meet us there. I have a couple of questions for him. Besides, I want to know if they've found the dog-nappers yet."

Que-tip salutes Bridget and with a twirl of her little body and a flash of pink sparkles, she's gone.

Bridget points her light along the track to her left, and it is barricaded at the tunnel's mouth. The tracks are definitely not being used in that direction. She points the light along the track to her right. She can make out the walls of the tunnel a good distance from where she is standing. They are black with soot and age.

"Did you check out the tracks?" She asks Mick.

"I did, I followed them for quite a bit. I had just come to a fork where two tracks meet up when I heard you cry out."

"Were there any signs of recent activity or people?"

"I used the dog form, and I could not smell the presence of people but with the other smells of oil and debris, it is hard to be one hundred that no one passed this way recently."

"Did you reach another station?"

"I saw signal lights ahead. I think there may be another station a half of a kilometer from where I turned back."

"We have to know for sure. Do you know of any magic that will heal my ankle so that I can jump down on the track and check it out myself?" Bridget asks.

Mick gives her a puzzled, questioning look and shakes his head. "Bridget, what is needed is for you to rest. Stay out of trouble, study the books I have given you and learn all the magic that you may be capable of."

"Thank you, Doctor Mick. That does not help. Didn't you hear Peter; we need to help him now."

"He also said that you need to rest and ice your ankle. Then you will be okay in a day or two."

"Mick, we may not have a day or two."

"There now, calm down. We will help him. Go over to the crate and sit down. You should not be standing."

Mick walked a few feet to a large crate that she'd not noticed before. It looked like the wooden box that the fruit vendor had his oranges in. It looks solid enough to hold her. Bridget hops over and sits down.

"Funny I didn't see this here before." She smiles as she recognizes the crate that was filled with rotten fruit. Knowing Mick, that store owner will be surprised to find his store filled with fresh produce in payment for the crate.

Mick ignores her and continues lecturing, "You will never learn all that you are capable of unless you spend some quiet time. This injury is a blessing in disguise. You must take care until you have learned to shield yourself from the evil creatures out to get revenge. Without full knowledge of your gifts, you will not be safe."

"Can you tell me how to set a shield in place now while we are waiting?"

"Close your eyes and try to still and calm your mind as I have taught you. Stillness is not easy to bring forth with the pain you are experiencing from your ankle. It will help if you breathe slowly and deeply... The major thing you must never do is panic. Panic brings fear and fear stops the mind from working properly."

Back at the flat, Bridget looks around at the four anxious faces staring at her. "Peter, I forgot to tell you that I invited another guest to help us. One person that you may not be able to see, he is a spirit, and his name is Friar Xavier. He is the spiritual guardian of the Royal family."

Peter looks to his left, "Pleased to meet you, Friar," and holds out his hand.

Bridget nods to Peter that the Friar is on his right. "That's okay Peter; the Friar is not used to shaking hands."

She explains to the Friar about Peter and his visions, and how important it is to get protection for the Cathedral. "Friar, does the Queen attend service at St. Paul's?"

The Friar is flying around the room and wringing his hands. He lands before

Bridget and in a begging voice asks, "You must stop this madman, our dear Queen cannot be hurt."

Bridget wishes she could give him a hug. He looks so worried, "I will do my very best, but we all must do our part to stop these terrorists."

"Of course, we must keep calm and carry on, right you are dear. Now where were we, yes, in answer to your question, our dear Queen does attend St. Paul's on occasion."

"Do you know if she plans on attending service at St. Paul's in the near future?"

Now it's Peter's turn for a panic attack. His mouth drops open and he stammers, "No Bridget, it can't be. I thought we decided that St. Paul's would be destroyed for shock value."

"Sorry Peter but I had a vision that leads me to believe killing the Queen is part of the whole picture."

"What vision?" Asked four voices at once.

Bridget explains what happened in the tube station. Of course leaving out the part where she sees herself shot. "I believe I may have seen the man in the tunnel in a recent picture. He is standing with the Royal family."

Friar Xavier sits on the edge of her bed, missing her foot by inches but she still feels a slight chill. Again wringing his hands and shaking his head. "Here I thought we were on the way to solving one mystery, and now we are looking for a would-be assassin, this is too much for one spirit."

They talk over all of the angles, and Bridget notices Peter slumping in his chair. He looks ready to fall asleep.

"Peter, please go home and rest. You can take the car. I'll be okay, honestly, how can I get into any trouble with these three babysitters?"

"Okay, only if you promise to rest yourself. I will call you tomorrow. Is there anything else I can get you?"

Bridget is lying on her bed with her foot on two fluffy pillows. Next to her is the TV clicker, a bottle of Coke, a pitcher of water, today's paper, a stack of magazines, surrounded by Mick, Que-tip, and Friar Xavier.

"No Peter, I'm sure I won't need anything else for the next twenty-four hours. Please go home and rest."

"Goodnight then."

"Goodnight," he calls out still looking guilty about leaving her. "I'll lock the door behind me."

"Thank you, Peter. Goodnight."

When she hears the door close, Bridget attempts to get up, and then hears Mick and Que-tip say, "No."

"Hey guys, give me a break will ya? I have to go to the bathroom." She can stand, but walking or even hopping is a hassle.

Suddenly she feels a cold arm holding her. She realizes how much effort it took for Friar Xavier to manifest in order to help her walk, "Thank you, Friar. I'm okay. You could do me a big favor and check on what dates the Queen is expected to attend St. Paul's."

She hops again and almost makes it to the door and then thinks of something else. "I would also like the names of those attending. Perhaps I can research them on Google. Could you also check on Michelle? I'm so worried about her. I need to know if they found the Dorgis. I bet the Queen is worried sick."

"Oh goodness, Her Majesty, of course, I will check on her right off, and let you know her itinerary straight away."

Bridget almost fell again when the Friar vanishes, but Mick moved a chair under her, and she sits down quickly.

Mick as Lord Howth, smiles down at her, "That was fast thinking; I would like to see what excuse you use to get rid of Que-tip."

"Perhaps there is a way to make a wizard disappear," Que-tip snipes.

"Stop it you two. I'm going to take a quick shower, and go to bed, so both of you, please put a sock in it." Bridget stands, and limps into the bathroom, trying to look as dignified as she can pulling a chair along. She hears Que-tip and Mick arguing over where they need to put socks, and chuckles.

Chapter 13

Bridget's Apartment
Battersea, England

"Come on in Peter. I'm out back in the garden."

Bridget is happy to hear Peter's voice sound much stronger this morning. Finding the tunnel entrance helped him feel as though he's getting closer to solving this very important case.

Bridget looks up as he enters the garden and smiles. Great man, is that a bakery box?

"Can I get you a cup of tea, the kettle is still hot?" Bridget asks.

"You stay sitting, I will help myself. Would you like a cup? I brought us some cupcakes from the Hummingbird Bakery. I heard that they are famous for American style baked goods and thought you might like some."

"Yes please, I would love one."

The morning is glorious; the fog has burned off, and the day is now bright and sunny. Bridget lays back in the lounge chair and enjoys the early morning sounds. Peter carries out a tray with his tea cup and a fresh hot pot of tea for both of them. She pours some cool tea into a thimble for Que-tip.

"Thank you for the cupcakes, I don't believe I ever had a cupcake that tastes like a cinnamon bun before, this is wonderful."

"It is my pleasure. How are you feeling? You do look much better."

"I have not been allowed to do much except rest and relax. My ankle feels much better. I'm sure I can walk on it with no problem."

Mick appears and takes one of the least sugary looking baked goods from the box. "Bridget, you look happy. Do you have some good news?"

"I have some great news. I think I know who is behind this attack."

"How? Did you call the yard?" Peter asks.

"No, not yet. Last night I mentioned the guy in my vision..."

Peter nods, and moves his cupcake, in a gesture to go on.

"I'd seen him someplace, but couldn't remember where. I've only been here at the house and playing tourist. So I took another look at all of the magazines and newspapers that are stacked for recycling, and then I found it."

"Who is he?" Peter asks.

"I think it might be Prince Oama Hassin; it looks a lot like him."

"Who?" Mick and Que-tip ask.

"Prince Oama is the older brother that had to stay at home with the family and be trained to take over the country as the future Amir. I think he plans on taking out the Queen, and the Cathedral. My guess is that he doesn't like the English, has a grudge against this country and his brother."

"Who is the brother?" Mick asks.

"Prince Ahmed Hassin, he's younger by a few years. He was born in his country, and then sent, when he was a young kid, to boarding schools in England. He sounds like he loves all things English. Including the women... He is marrying an Englishwoman."

"Is that why they were in the news?" Peter asks, "The wedding?"

"That's it. The article on 'The Royals' highlighted the upcoming wedding. The bride is a minor English royal; the Queen is her Godmother. The Queen and many of the royal families plan to attend. The young Prince wants to strengthen ties between his small country and the English people. He plans to do that by going against his local custom and marrying an Englishwoman, and in a church."

"That church is St. Paul's?" Mick sits down on Bridget's lounger.

"You got it. The article did not give the wedding date. I asked Friar Xavier to look at the Queen's social calendar. He should be here soon."

Everyone is talking at once. Michelle has come to tell Bridget her good news. Bridget introduces Michelle to Peter who stands and offers her his chair. She smiles and thanks him and then proceeds, in a rush of words to tell them how miraculous it is that the wonderful, handsome,

Inspector Boyle, had uncovered evidence in the rubble at the old kennel site, which led the police to the culprits. The suspected culprits and their homes are under observation, and the evidence against Michelle's participation in the dognapping was so thin; her solicitor was able to convince the authorities to let her go home. Of course, she was warned not to leave the area.

Mick and Que-tip are arguing about the tracks, and Friar Xavier is trying to get her attention. Bridget is getting a major headache. Why did she ever believe it was a gift to hear spirits and the fae folk? She can't openly speak with them with Michelle around. She has to get rid of Michelle but how?

"I'm so glad that you're no longer under arrest. I just knew they were wrong. You could never have taken the dogs. I think the Queen will want to apologize to you personally, as soon as the dogs are found."

Everyone stops talking and stares at Bridget as if she is crazy. She silently tells them, *"Trust me, guys; it is way too complicated to bring Michelle into this whole St. Paul's thing."*

"You know the best way to enjoy your new found freedom?" Bridget asks.

"Pardon?" A puzzled Michelle asks.

"A shopping trip!"

Michelle squeaks and jumps up from where she is sitting with Peter. "*Oui*, I have seen the perfect dress…"

Bridget stands up to move towards her and yells, "Ouch, this darn ankle." She'll never win an academy award for her acting, but Peter is so guilt ridden for bringing her into the tunnel that he doesn't notice.

"Bridgette, you are hurt. I forgot." Michelle thumps her forehead with the palm of her hand. "No, no, how bad of me, I cannot go shopping. I will not think of leaving you. I must stay with you and be your Florence."

"My what?" Bridget asks.

"The famous Englishwoman, she started the whole nursing industry. Without her women would probably not even be doctors today."

Bridget nods, "Now I remember learning about her in school. She was named Florence because she was born in Florence, Italy. I love reading biographies of famous women; Florence Nightingale was my favorite." *Was she the spirit I met on the train? Why would she appear to me?*

Bridget looks at Michelle and yawns. "Please don't think you need to stay. You would be so bored. I'm going back to bed. Michelle, I believe you need to be prepared. Think of all of those cameras and dignitaries. You must look your best. I have it; Peter will take you. I have a rental car, and I can't use it. He can drive you to the shops. It would be a favor to me since I can't do anything today anyway." Bridget looks at Peter and hopes he will understand and leave with Michelle.

"Are you certain Bridget?" He asks.

"Yes, Peter. I promise. I won't get into any trouble resting." Mick snorts, Peter looks around, but Mick, Que-tip, and Friar Xavier are invisible, Peter and Michelle can't see them.

After a lot more fussing, Peter getting ice and Michelle making her more tea, Bridget is finally able to get them both to leave.

Bridget sighs when the front door closes. "Okay Friar, do you have the social calendar of the Queen?"

Friar Xavier looks at the nightstand by her bed and in a few seconds, a flash of brilliant light appears, leaving behind an old fashioned, leather bound, handwritten journal.

"Friar, you didn't take the real one, did you?"

"No, my dear that is just a copy."

"Wow, that sure beats Xerox." Bridget jumps up off the bed and is pushed back down by three very determined entities. "Hey guys, relax, I'm fine. I was just trying to get rid of Michelle and Peter. He needs to cool it. He is so nervous he's making me crazy and hey, they make a cute couple."

Bridget runs her finger down the list of entries and finds one entitled, 'Lady Margaret Chaternning's wedding, S.P.C. at 10 A.M.' "Well guys, it looks like we only have five days before the wedding. If I were the terrorists, I would not lay the bomb too early for fear it would be detected. They also cannot wait until the last minute. I think we need to go back down there today."

A worried Mick asks, "Bridget, are you really up to another long walk? I am reluctant to have any of us use much magic for fear of calling attention to Morrigan's followers."

If only he knew, they have tried several times already. "Don't worry Mick; I will call a taxicab to take us right to the entrance of the old tube station. We know the way in, it won't be so hard. Hey, this is a piece of cake!" She burst out laughing at the puzzled looks on all three faces. She loves using old expressions; their interpretations were priceless.

Bridget dresses in her all black, 'cat burglar' outfit and gathers her tools and two flashlights. She has called the cab company and was all set to leave when it arrives.

The cab brings them to the alley entrance. She can't help but notice the crowd of people shopping at the fruit vendor and smiles at Mick.

The street is crowded but walking a dog is always a good excuse to turn into an alley. Talking Mick into appearing as a dog took a while, but finally, he gave in. The way is clear, and soon they are inside the old station.

Bridget remembers to hug the wall. Friar and Que-tip go on ahead to make sure that they are alone. Mick stays close, and this time, she is smart enough to wear leather gloves and can hold onto the wall with no bad vibes. Just as she is about to jump down onto the tracks, she has an overwhelming sense of fear. What the heck was she thinking? She heard stories of what they call the third rail; maybe it's electrified.

"Bridget, please calm down. Take a deep breath. You cannot let your fears guide your life. If you ever want to achieve anything in this life, you must let go of your fears."

"There you go again listening in on my thoughts. I thought we talked about this. My thoughts are off limits. Get it? Of course, I'm worried about dying. You don't have that worry. You have what, nine lives?"

"That is said about cats, in case you have not noticed, I am a dog."

Bridget laughs as Mick intends and says, "Okay, let's get going. You know, you are wrong about fear, sometimes a good sense of fear keeps you alive."

Bridget jumps down onto the tracks and prays the twinge in her ankle will stop soon. She has way too much to do to let pain get in her way.

Her heavy duty flashlight lights up the tunnel, and she notices the 'third rail' and keeps far away from it, just in case. They walk for what feels like ten city blocks when they see a very bright light coming their way. Bridget runs back to where she noticed a cut out in the wall that may have at one time held maintenance equipment. Just before she enters it, she hears, "Bridget we found something interesting."

She turns back; Friar and Que-tip are lit up like two bright searchlights. "Wow, turn those lights down a little, I can't see you."

"Sorry my dear, little Miss Que-tip has some amazing talents." Friar Xavier explains.

"Why didn't you mention that the other day?" Bridget asks.

"I did not want to let the creeps know we were down here, and they may have noticed my light. This time, I checked out the tunnel, it is clear, so I turned on my high beams."

Bridget laughs at her expression. "Good job. What did you find?"

"Just ahead a bit, the tunnel bears to the right. Friar checked it out, and the track on the right goes under the Cathedral. Further along, the left track you come to the Exchange."

"The Exchange, that is like our 'Wall Street,' like in the stock exchange?"

"Righto," Mick says sounding for once very British.

"Is there any sign that anyone has been down here?"

"Nothing we can spot. Some very old traces of people, litter, graffiti, and things like that, nothing recent."

They all walk or in Que-tip and Friar Xavier case, fly down to where the tunnel split. Only one track went to the right and one to the left. Bridget wonders how they managed the schedule of train service back then. *I guess fewer people meant fewer trains.*

"Mick if you can't smell recent traces of people, then we still may have time. If they haven't been down here yet, then they don't know of the split. One of the military guys the other night told us a story of a

Bernadette Crepeau

British stage magician; he was a famous magician or what they called an Illusionist who they used during the war to trick the Germans. I think we can do the same thing. George mentioned a new type of camouflage that the military uses. If we can get it, we can hang it from the ceiling and completely cover the opening that leads under the Cathedral."

"Minor problem, they will see the tracks leading that way." Mick states.

"Not if we remove them," Bridget explains.

"Que-tip, you once told me that some of your mates have special gifts. Can any of them lift heavy weights? Do you think that they can remove the track that goes to the right?"

"They may need some help. Faeire gifts are more to empower others with strength when they need it the most. You ever hear of a frail, ninety-pound mother, lifting a car that was about to come down on her child? Well, that is one of us giving her the power when she needs it most. That is the type of thing that we do."

Bridget smiles and says, "I know just the frail, ninety-pound folks they can work with, let's walk to the area under the Exchange; there is something I need to check out."

They walk the track until they are under the Exchange. They then go back to the place where the track splits and walk until they are under the Cathedral. It is about the same distance.

Bridget claps her hands in excitement. "This may work. It is crazy guys, but it just may work."

When they arrive home, a very tired and worried cousin is waiting for them. Bridget hurries to explain where they have been and what her plan is.

"Peter, don't look so worried, it'll work. Remember the other night at the British Legion; George told us the story of Jasper Maskelyne, the British stage magician in the 1930s and 40s."

"Yes, his 'Magic Gang' built a number of tricks. They used painted canvas and plywood to make jeeps look like tanks — with fake tank tracks — and tanks look like trucks. They created illusions of armies and battleships. But Bridget, make an entire tunnel disappear? We don't have Jasper around anymore."

"Jasper's largest trick was to conceal Alexandria and the Suez Canal by misdirecting the German bombers. He built a mockup of the night-lights of Alexandria in a bay three miles away with fake buildings, lighthouse, and anti-aircraft batteries. To mask the Suez Canal, he built a revolving cone of mirrors that created a wheel of spinning light nine miles wide, meant to dazzle and disorient enemy pilots so that their bombs would fall off-target. Heck, all we have to worry about is a tunnel."

"Piece of Pie!" Shouts Que-tip.

"That's a piece of cake," Bridget laughs, "but Que-tip is right, we can do this. All you need to do is to convince the veterans, and I will go and speak with the faeire."

"How on earth can we do this?" A confused Peter asks.

Bridget laughs at the expression on his face. "I will explain all the details later, I promise." *I hope my ideas all fall into place, so this plan makes sense.*

She looks around at an excited Que-tip and some very worried guys. "Okay guys, have a little faith. We don't have much time. They will try to set the bombs soon. I will also need to let my friend Charlie in on this. Hopefully, he won't have me put into the loony bin and throw away the key."

Chapter 14

Stonehenge
Amesbury, England

Friar Xavier accompanies Peter to the Battersea British Legion. Que-tip goes to round up her faeire friends.

Mick and Bridget head to the fae meeting place at Stonehenge. They take the ramp onto Knightsbridge A4 and soon merge onto the M3. Bridget feels proud that she is not only finding her way around England but also driving on the left side of the road. She does great, but Mick still groans and covers his eyes at every roundabout. "I know we must stop Morrigan followers from coming after you, but this mortal transportation may be more dangerous. Careful now, there must be a bloody roundabout every mile or so," Mick complains.

"It's getting dark. I hope we get there soon. I don't know why you insist that I don't use magic in England. Isn't that why I am learning it. I could just zap us to where we want to go."

"As I explained we must keep you safe. If word gets out that you are in England, then you will need to return to Ireland so that we can protect you from Morrigan's evil followers that want revenge."

Bridget almost shouts that they know it already and have attempted to kill her, but she wants to stay in England, so she remains quiet.

They finally spot the sign for the Junction Eight exit towards Salisbury. Que-tip materializes on the dashboard just as Bridget is pulling out of another roundabout. She jams on the brakes and pulls to the side of the road.

Mike growls. "Next time, ear wax, give a person a warning or something."

Bridget takes a deep breath to calm her nerves, "Were you able to reach the others?"

"Sure, they are all waiting for you. Stay on this road and I will show you a back way in to avoid the tourists."

"But it's dark already, won't they be gone?"

"You must be kidding mate. Night-time is when things heat up around here. There are always those who want to dance naked among the stones and the local constable has his hands full."

By the time Bridget stops the car its pitch black. She looks around her. *Funny how truly dark the country is without any lights from buildings or street lights.* She turns off the car and steps out onto a rocky, grass field. She stands for a moment to let her eyes adjust to the dark.

The night feels perfect. She can smell flowers of some kind, and there is a mild breeze that brings warm air and a hint of music. Someone is playing the flute it sounds magical. The peaceful sound sweeps around her and takes away all the doubts of her plan succeeding.

Bridget feels wrapped in a cocoon of peace. She looks up at the stars and just then a meteor streaks across the sky, leaving a trail of glittering light behind. *Wow, what a rush. I feel incredible; I wonder what's happening? Am I feeling the magic of Stonehenge?*

Que-tip's little body lights up with a soft glow and points the way. They walk for several minutes and stand beside a rock wall.

"Better size down for the entrance you two," Que-tip suggests.

"Size down?" Bridget asks.

"Don't tell me you have not mastered that yet." Que-tip looks at Mick accusingly.

"I am getting to it. We must learn the basics first. Perhaps you could help her this time."

With a quick nod from Que-tip, Bridget is spinning. She feels dizzy but opens her eyes to look around.

She has entered a magical open air area filled with fae. The brilliant night sky is their ceiling, and the soft green grass is their dance floor. Several of the fae are walking around playing all sorts of instruments. Many of the ladies have flowers in their hair, and a lot of the guys wear Robin Hood type hats with feathers. Everything is rainbow-hued with vivid sparkling colors and bright, multicolored flashes as more faeire arrive with their sparkling wings spread.

"I was thinking of maybe a dozen fae, not hundreds," an astonished Bridget admits.

"They all gathered here to meet you and bring back word of you to their tribes," Que-tip explains.

"There are more?"

"Our numbers are strong. There are as many fae as there are humans, which is why we could not let Morrigan take control over all of us. She could have caused great damage to the future of humankind if she was left to continue."

A male faeire with sandy colored hair and bright blue eyes approaches and bows before Bridget. She looks around, and others are bowing.

Bridget is embarrassed by the fae bowing around her and says. "Guys please don't do that. I'm just here to meet you. I'm your guest."

"As the prophecy predicted, you not only came to us in our hour of need, but you defeated Morrigan. My name is Emanon; I am honored to meet you. I would like you to meet my second in command, David."

Emanon nods to a young man, with curly, black hair. He flies from the crowd and kneels before her.

Embarrassed by the kneeling, Bridget says, "Hey guys, please cut that out. It's making me feel weird."

Emanon nods and David stands. He's a little taller than her in this short form and so cute. Like Que-tip, his pointed ears are covered by his hair and his dark-brown eyes tilt just a little bit. The most noticeable difference between him and Emanon is his elfin face; it has mischief written all over it.

David bends his knee and removes a pointed hat with a very long feather, and sweeps it to his side. "Welcome, my Lady."

Bridget couldn't help it; she bursts out laughing. "Sorry guys, but you look like you just stepped out of casting for a Three Musketeers movie. You also don't need to bow before me; I'm not royalty."

They hear a loud gasp, and everyone starts speaking at once. Mick comes over and stands next to her and says, "Attention fae!"

Mick isn't speaking very loud, but everyone is silent again.

"Bridget does not consider herself royalty. Although as we all know, she is of royal descent and is royalty. In her country, the United States of America, all people are equal. Hence her discomfort with being recognized as, how shall we say, special."

She hears a noise like leaves rustling in the trees, feels a strong breeze and looks around. *Wow, what an incredible sight, the Fae are clapping their wings.*

She has seen the fae land with wings outspread, as soon as they touch land they absorb their wings back into their bodies, as she has often seen Que-tip do. Now with all the wings on view, the room takes on the look of a pirates' treasure chest, flowing over with precious jewels.

She moves further into the room that resembles a crystal cave. "I'm very happy to meet all of you. My name is Bridget. My friend Mick here is the one who taught me all that I needed to help the fae."

They all applaud again, and Bridget listens to the happy music and looks at the beautiful spectacle in front of her and as Mick would say 'she is living in the moment.'

The Fae celebrate Bridget's visit. Many play instruments as they float in the air or dance among the others. Bridget recognizes guitars, fiddles, and ukulele, harp, drums, and another that resembles a smaller version of a cello.

She watches entranced by the sights and sounds. Soon she can feel the music under her skin, and she also begins to laugh and dance. She feels great. She twirls around and moves to the beat of the joyful sounding Celtic music. She feels so carefree; she can't stop laughing.

She feels someone staring and looks at Mick. His normally golden eyes have taken on the color of warm honey. She wonders what he's thinking.

"My lady?"

"Me?"

"Yes, my lady. Please follow me, the council is ready to commence."

They enter a large alcove. She hears a swishing sound and a clear, transparent film closes behind them. This cover completely stops all sounds from the party a few feet away. She looks at the now serious faces forming a circle.

David begins the introductions. "As Emanon mentioned, in your language, I am called David. I coordinate the various council members and their activities. This lovely lady is Deirdre, she and Alan are my second in command."

Bridget looks at the dark haired pair. Both are smiling and obviously a couple. No wonder they share the position.

"This is Sam." A very handsome sandy-haired man bows before her. "I work with your warriors, my lady. This is Cade; he is our strategist." A young guy with light brown hair, sparkling eyes, and a beautiful smile comes over and bows.

The introductions continue. Half of their job duties Bridget can't remember and many of the names she can't pronounce. Then David turns to a group of girls so different from one another but all with the same confidence and strength she has become used to with Que-tip.

Before he could continue with introductions, Que-tip speaks up, "Bridget, these are my mates; Brandie, Brittney, Regan, Kearin, Samantha, Lindsey, Leonda, Tracey, Annie and Kasondra. We are in communications."

Deirdre looks puzzled, "RaeAnne, we are, all of us, in communications."

Aha, now I know Que-tips real name.

"I should have said that we are experts in communications. We encourage others to get the job done and done right." They all giggle.

David speaks up, "We hear that you are in need of illusionists, these men are the ones for the job." She looks over at three young guys who resemble each other. "This is John, Joseph, and Thomas."

"Are they really illusionists?" Bridget asks.

"No, but they are not afraid of hard work and will do whatever needs to be done to help you create an illusion."

"Thank you all for meeting with me. I need all of your help. As Mick mentioned, I'm still learning. There are so many skills that mortals are born with, that we don't even know we have because we seldom use them.

I'm being offered challenges that I would not normally face, for the opportunity to realize what gifts I have. And to gain the confidence to reach for other gifts that may be available. The more I use my gifts, the more confidence I will gain. With that confidence will come the strength to help us defeat what Morrigan follows are left. What I am facing now is a mortal challenge. Not only is a major spiritual symbol being threatened but we may also be facing a threat to the life of the Queen and all of the Royal Family..."

Bridget speaks with the fae for several hours. Exhaustion is setting in. She feels Mick nudge her mind.

"You're right Mick. I've got to get home. Que-tip, could you fill them in on anything I missed. Goodnight everyone. Thank you again for your help."

A couple of faeire appear and show Mick and Bridget the way out. They find themselves back under the magnificent ceiling of stars and back to normal size.

"Thank you. I don't feel as tired now; guess the cold air woke me up." Bridget stumbles a few times but with the light provided by the faeire, they find the car.

"Thanks again, please say goodnight to everyone."

As Bridget drives back to Battersea, she talks the plan over with Mick. "The fae we met with are young. We can only hope that Cade is up to the strategy that will be needed to do battle. I really liked him. He is cute and smart. I think he will live up to any challenge we give him."

"They may appear young but compared to you, they are ancient," Mick laughs.

Bridget is quiet and dares not think about the age difference between her and Mick for fear he reads her thoughts. She blinks rapidly to keep back the tears.

Chapter 15

Bridget's Apartment
Battersea, England

"What time is it Mick?"

"Straight up ten."

"Ten! Mick, why on earth did you let me sleep so long? We have a lot to do today!"

"You need your rest. Have a cup of tea and you won't be so grumpy."

"Peter should be here by now, where is he?"

"He will be here soon."

Bridget jumps up and runs into the bathroom. "Thank goodness; my ankle is back to normal. I have so much to do today. I have to meet with Peter and the Vets from the legion. I have to remember to tell Peter that many of the fae will meet us in the tube station so he won't be surprised. They will be able to help lift objects that our guys would not be able to on their own. I hope that the old timers were able to recruit some young guys to help also."

When the doorbell rings, she answers it while towel drying her hair. She opens the door to find Peter standing there with six guys in their late twenties. The hunks have elite military stamped all over them from the way they are standing and the haircuts. Behind them is a large black Humvee.

"Yikes, come on in, I will be back in a moment." Bridget rushes back into her bedroom and mumbles, "Great; I finally meet some cute guys, and I look like a cartoon character with her 'fuzzy bunny' slippers and old fuzzy housecoat. She looks up at Que-tip on top of the wardrobe. "Cut that out; I can hear you giggle. It's not funny, how can I boss those guys around after they have seen me like this?"

"Ah, get over yourself. They will listen to you because you are smart and know what you are talking about, not how you look. Go out there like the one in charge and you will be." Que-tip orders.

Bridget quickly puts on her old jeans, sweatshirt, and sneakers. The front parlor is small, but she never realized how small until it is filled with seven guys and Mick, now in dog form. They stop talking when she walks in and are staring at her chest. *Okay, I know I have a good size chest, but it has never stopped a room full of men talking.* She is about to run back to the bedroom when she hears Mick laugh.

"Bridget me darling, what does that say on your shirt?"

She looks down to see what top she put on in her rush and laughs. "Hi guys, this is a word we say a lot back home 'Forgetaboutit.'"

They all laugh. Peter comes over, puts his arm around her shoulder and introduces her. "Bridget these guys are just back from the Stan, enjoying some R&R in London. Guys, meet my wonderful Yankee cousin, Bridget."

She whispers to Peter, "How much have you told them? Do they think we are crazy?"

"No, Luv, no worry, worked on a case with Fred here a while back. He knows that when I say something will happen, it usually does." Peter nods to a young man, barely her height of five foot, five inches, but he is all muscle. His hair is cut so short he looks bald. "I'm Fred Miss. I can vouch for him. My mates and I have just the thing to get the job done."

"Great, you found some net?"

"Better than ordinary net, we have some Vizzy-Cloth, think you yanks call it Camo-cloak. Good stuff. It reflects the light, causing an optical illusion. The blokes will think they are looking at another tunnel wall. We will turn them around; that's for certain."

"That's so cool. Okay, guys, let's get started. *Mick and Que-tip, once we get there, please go on ahead of us and make sure that we don't meet up with anyone.*"

"Fred, you and Bridget take her car. I will hop in the Humvee with the guys and show them the way." Peter is on a roll now. He no longer looks tired. He is doing something he loves, helping people in trouble. Bridget is enjoying herself also. She knows that this is dangerous, but is happy to be helping.

Peter leads the guys into the tunnel and explains their plan. Bridget waits at the entrance for the vets from the legion hall. When they arrive, she is very surprised to see George has Maggie with them. They are out of breath. She should have driven over to get them. *Hope they didn't walk all the way.*

"Okay girlie this is all of us that could make it. Did the guys from The Duke of Lancaster's 1st Battalion meet up with Pete?"

"Yes, they are in the tunnel now. Let's go inside, so we don't attract too much attention, and I'll let you know the plan."

One guy with an unlit pipe kept shaking his head. "Do you have a question, Lloyd?" Bridget asks.

"Why don't you call in the yard for this? We are old; we can't be any help."

"You have already helped. We have the guys you sent over working now. They will hang a curtain to block off the entrance to the tunnel that goes under St. Paul's. Once we have the track removed that leads to that tunnel, no one will ever know it was there. That is when I will contact a friend at the yard and let him know that I think the Exchange is in danger. Hopefully, the yard will set up surveillance and catch the guys in the act."

"Why can't they set up surveillance under St. Paul's?" Lloyd asks.

"I thought of that, but I may not be believed, and I don't want to take the chance."

It looks as though Lloyd is going to argue some more but just then Maggie starts laughing. It's so unexpected they all join in.

"The Yank has it right. They may think she's bonkers and ignore her over the church but do you think they will take a chance if someone threatens to mess with the country's money?"

Bridget had brought a small step ladder, so no one had to jump onto the track. Peter's crew had also brought crowbars, torches to cut the track into smaller movable pieces, and wooden boxes the vets could sit on.

Bridget nods to the fae, each of the vets had company on their shoulders, but the fae can cloak so as not to be seen. Que-tip had explained to her that this ability comes close to the 'age of reason.' Before that, it can be done, but it takes a great deal of energy.

The fae are to 'suggest' to the vets the best place to cut the track and then assist them. Peter's crew would also help lift the track beyond the curtain. The vets would then take turns sweeping away any remaining traces of track left behind.

Bridget stays by Lloyd and helps him cut his first section of track. After the guys move his section, they take a break and sit on the platform.

Lloyd puts his unlit pipe in his mouth and tells her, "I haven't done that much work in a long time. Didn't know I had it in me. I worked in the shipyards most of my life, welding mostly. I have always been fascinated by trains. Did you know that our own Metropolitan Line was the first underground railway system in the world? Built in 1863 it was."

"I didn't know that, thank you, I love history. I thought people were still in the horse and buggy stage around then. Some of the cities on the west coast of our country were not even settled by 1863." Bridget visits with Lloyd a few more minutes and then walks around to check on their progress. Two guys are up at the ceiling hammering in metal stakes to hold the curtain in place. Que-tip and her mates are keeping an eye on any possible opening where unexpected guests might catch them in action. Peter is busy with two guys further along the tunnel to St. Paul's.

Bridget calls out to him. "How's it going, Peter?"

As Peter walks towards Bridget, he answers, "The guys did not find anything. They have a device that informs them if any charges are in this area. It is clean."

Peter leans closer and whispers, "Mick hasn't found any traces of humans since our last visit. Bridget, what if I am all wrong. What if it is not in a tunnel?"

"When the tunnel project is complete, why not ask the guys to make a sweep of the church, better safe than sorry."

"Good idea."

Bridget holds her flashlight in front of her to watch where she is walking and goes deeper into the tunnel. She feels on edge again. *What's wrong with me, besides the fact that I think a terrorist will shoot me, or I'll be killed by one of Morrigan's followers? There it is again, that feeling of being watched.*

She swings her light to the left and just sees a black soot covered rock wall. She swings her light to the right and feels the hair on the back of her neck stand up. The light illuminates the black soot wall but it is blacker in one area, and that area has the shape of a small dwarf who is now holding a flaming arrow.

She does the only smart thing she can think of; she runs as fast as possible back to people. Unfortunately, she does the 'trip over your own feet' thing and lands with a crash. She feels it before she sees it, a blast of fire. She can feel the heat on her face. She buries her face in her hands and cries out, "Mick, I need you! Help!"

Within seconds, Mick and Que-tip materialize next to her.

"Stay down!" Mick orders.

Que-tip flies to Bridget's back and takes out her bow and arrow. If she weren't so scared, she'd laugh, she has seen toothpicks bigger than that arrow.

Mick examines the wall where the dark shadow was and then the wall that the flame hit.

Bridget sits up, "I'm surprised no one else is here, I would imagine panic would set in with a flame that size."

"I was able to sprinkle them all with a time spell. They will not see it," Que-tip explains.

"A time spell, hey that's real cool."

"Bridget, you really must study more magic. What is also cool is what I can do with this little toothpick, want me to show you?"

"Oops, sorry about that Que-tip, it's just laughter taking the place of the hysterics I don't have time for."

"Whoever it was, did not leave a trail. I know one thing, this villain is not human. Morrigan's followers know you are in the area."

"Great. I don't have time for this," Bridget sighs.

"It is their way. They want revenge. Lucky for us there is only a few left. They did a poor job of it; that assassin was probably a trainee."

"Thanks a lot. If I didn't trip, he would have succeeded. That flame would have hit me directly. Good thing I'm clumsy. I was so scared I even forgot to set the protective shield in place."

Que-tip and Mick exchange a look.

"So out with it, what's with the look?"

"Bridget there are no accidents. Often what we cry over is just something minor that has happened to prevent something major happening."

"Like I have a bruised body instead of being a fried crispy critter?"

"Exactly! Bridget even though you may not have remembered to protect yourself, your instincts kicked in and raised the shield. The heat you felt was the flame striking the shield. Que-tip and I can see the marks of flame all around you."

"That thing hit me?" She shakes off the fear the only way she knows, "Okay guys, enough rest, time to get back to work. Do you think we can finish this today?"

Mick looks at Bridget, *How can you not love someone who puts helping others before her own safety.*

As if she has read his thoughts, Que-tip says, "We will finish. You and Mick are to return home."

"But Que-tip, I need...?"

"We are close to our goal. Do you think the fae want you in harm's way?"

"Okay, but make sure you have the vets rest every fifteen minutes or so. I know you guys are doing all the work, but I don't want anything happening to them and make sure Peter sends them home in a cab, okay?"

"It will be done. Now go home and work with Mick to strategize how you will defeat these Morrigan followers out for revenge."

"Yeah, I hear ya. Nothing too difficult, just stop the 'Goddess of War's followers, yeah, yeah, yeah, easy for you to say."

Bridget knows Que-tip is right. She has been keeping busy with this to avoid dealing with the bigger picture. Someone wants to kill her. She has had too many 'accidents' happen lately, the chair at the Spa, the guy in the tube station. Maybe her assailant was influenced by one of Morrigan's followers and then had a change of mind. She doesn't know. That is the big problem; she doesn't know what to expect. She doesn't know what is coming next or who it may be. Morrigan's evil could have influenced anyone who is not strong in their own beliefs.

Chapter 16

Bridget's Apartment
Battersea, England

He's close. He's carrying a light in his left hand and in its glow I can see him. He is tall. I can see the sleeve of his jacket. It is red and shiny, like satin. It has embroidery in gold, very exotic. He's...

"Bridget, wake up."

"Darn it, Mick; I almost saw him up close this time. I know him, at least I'm pretty sure it is the guy in the magazine I pointed out."

"Who?"

"The guy who's going to blow up the church, that's who, you know, the brother of the guy that's getting married."

"I think it is time you tell me again of this vision."

"You're right," Bridget tells Mick what happened when she fell on the stairs at the station. She leaves off the part where she is shot. *I can't tell him. He and Que-tip will pack me away to a deserted island, and I have to finish this.*

Bridget shivers, "I'm having all kinds of nightmares and encounters with evil fae...."

"What other encounters have you had that you are not telling me about?" An upset Mick asks.

She watches as Friar Xavier materializes next to her bed. "Bridget, I hope I am not interrupting."

She feels Mick stiffen and realizes she has her arm around him. Holding onto him for comfort has become a habit. Holding or petting an animal always made her feel good, but holding Mick makes her feel something very special.

"That's okay Friar; we were just talking about my nightmare. How are things at the Palace?" She asks.

"That is why I am here." There was a quick flash on the bed next to her, and her nerves must be worse than she thought. She squeezes Mick too hard, and he says, "Take care, it is only the good Friar, and his magic."

"Sorry Mick." She picks up a fancy envelope. "What's this Friar?"

"You may wish to attend the reception for the wedding party. If one has an invitation, it is much easier to enter. The Hotel will be heavily guarded."

Bridget opens a heavy vellum envelope lined with gold foil. The invitation embossed with a royal crest, and the lettering is also in gold.

"Yikes, it'll be held at the Savoy on the Strand. I could see it when I took a ride on the London's Eye Ferris Wheel. It's beautiful. I'd love to go, but I can't."

Mick nods his head in agreement, "You are finally getting some common sense."

"What do you mean Mick?" Asks a concerned Friar.

"Sorry Friar, Bridget had an encounter today with one of Morrigan's henchman. She is too frightened to go."

"I am not too frightened to go anywhere. I just don't belong there. I will never fit in and what on earth would I wear?" She could tell that Mick was frowning, and Friar Xavier was smiling, but she refused to look at them.

"Well, I guess it would be good to see the wedding party up close. I might be able to sense who the villains are. Maybe I

♣ 200 ♣

could get an outfit that doesn't cost too much. There is that resale shop in the East End that I want to check out. What do you think?"

Mick reluctantly admits, "You should be safe there. Perhaps your gift will allow you to determine who the villains are, and we could watch to see when they enter the tunnel."

She looks at the date on the invite. "Yikes, I only have a few days. I have to call Michelle, time to go shopping."

"Why call Michelle?"

"An important outfit like this calls for girl time."

"Did I hear you say shopping?"

"Hi Que-tip, how are things in the tunnel?"

"The tracks are moved you cannot even tell they were there. The curtain is completely covering the tunnel entrance to St. Paul's. You would have to get close and actually feel the wall to realize it is not soot covered rock. It looks great. Enough of dark, dirty tunnels, I want to go shopping."

"Of course, you can come. I'll call Michelle."

Chapter 17

Bridget's Apartment
Battersea, England

Bridget quickly changes and just has time to grab her Coach handbag with Que-tip safely hidden away inside when Michelle arrives.

"Don't worry Mick. Morrigan's followers won't know that I'm still alive. It will take them awhile to find out and get another assassin lined up. Go back to Ireland; Que-tip will keep an eye on me."

She runs out the door almost knocking down Michelle before Mick continues demanding that he guards her on her shopping trip.

Michelle has her small Fiat parked out front, and they laughingly run through the morning drizzle.

"I love having my little car back from the police. Where do you wish to go first, Bridgette?"

"I hear that there are some great vintage pieces at The Oxfam Thrift Store. Let's try that first."

"Okay but I insist that if you do not find what you want there, that next stop is Kings Road in swinging Chelsea. The shops there are my favorite, and I have to show you where I found my outfit to meet the Queen."

Bridget silently prays that Friar Xavier has put a bug in the Queen's ear about meeting Michelle.

In The East End, she finds the perfect formal wedding reception outfit. Michelle picked it out. Bridget thinks it looks like a pretty floral prom dress. Michelle calls it perfect, the quintessentially English looking dress.

It does have that traditional English rose look. Never thought she would be wearing a white dress, covered in flowers but the strapless prom dress look, with a netting underskirt and pink sash tie. She even found a hat and matching shoes.

Michelle looks at her a little funny when she purchases the little flower girl crown, with tiny flowers and a long veil.

"Just a little something, I think a friend of mine will like."

Que-tip is sound asleep in her purse after wearing herself out, flying from one display to another. Thank goodness she was able to keep herself somewhat invisible. She wouldn't have stopped until Bridget told her she would buy the flower girl crown and warned her about seeing the shopkeeper grab a fly swatter.

They had fun shopping and a great lunch which Michelle treated her to before driving her back to Battersea.

Bridget calls out. "Mick, are you home?" She looks in the garden, but he's gone. She picks up a sleeping Que-tip and places her on her pillow and quietly closes the door.

She returns to the garden and lays in the sun. Enjoying the peace and quiet, she closes her eyes.

The scraping noise is coming closer. He's carrying a light. He's wearing a fancy outfit. He smiles. Her feet are frozen in place; she opens her mouth to yell for Mick, but no sound comes.

She hears a low growl. Shakes myself awake and rub her eyes. Her fingers come away wet.

"Sorry Mick, I must've fallen asleep. You know you are not a dog and need to stop that growling thing, right? But thanks for waking me, it was another nightmare. Did you have a good day?"

Chapter 18

Savoy on the Strand
London, England

Thank goodness for the lavish flower arrangements, they're everywhere, in urns and baskets, on the tables, pedestals, and even the floor. Bridget slips behind a large arrangement to avoid the welcoming line. She keeps talking to herself to calm her nerves. *My outfit looks okay; I can blend in. Just breathe.*

She looks at the crowd gathered in a beautiful glass room. The ceiling and walls are all glass and the plants that are not inside are framing the view of the gardens. She looks around at the who's who of royalty. She loves reading all of the fashion magazines and now feels she is in one. She can see Princess Victoria of Sweden, Queen Rania of Jordan, the Duchess of Essex and many more whose names she can't remember. All the beautiful, fancy, ultra-rich people. She can feel her heart race, turns and heads back to the door. *What on earth am I thinking? They'll find out that I'm a party crasher and lock me up. I don't belong here. Not only are these guys way out of my league but they're royalty for goodness sake.*

She is almost back to the entrance when she hears her mother's voice, *"Get back in there young lady. Do you think you are so high and mighty that you cannot sit with other folks? You think that they'll stop what they're doing just to look at you?"* She stops walking and starts laughing, just as she did when she heard those words ten years ago.

Her mother would take her once a month, in their Sunday best, to have a cup of tea at some swank hotel or restaurant in Manhattan. The first time her mother brought her she was sick to her stomach and ran out of the restaurant. Her mother knew she was lacking in confidence and felt that she was not good enough to sweep the floor in a fancy place, no mind sit down and drink tea.

Just as she did back then, she feels her mother put her arm through hers, and tell her to put her head up, and shoulders back. She would say, 'Remember young lady, God created you, He created me and all of those people in this fancy place. God makes no trash.'

Bridget dashes into the restroom and touches up her makeup. She misses her mother but knows she is with her. *I'll make her proud and help Peter do this.* She leaves the safety of the restroom and boldly walks over to the buffet line, fills her plate with a little of everything: lobster, pate, curry chicken, prime rib. *Wow, what a spread. No shortage of money in this crowd. There is no way I can eat all this, but it will give me an excuse not to talk to anyone.*

She just finishes the lobster when the people from the welcoming line take their seats. There are two dark-skinned, middle-eastern looking men sitting on either side of Lady Margaret. The young prince is holding her hand, looking so proud and happy, smiling at everyone. *Wow, what a catch, he's hot.*

She notices two things at once. The guy she assumes is his brother is not wearing glasses. He looks fierce and angry. He could be the older brother, but he doesn't look like the guy in the tunnel. *Darn, those two guys look a lot alike. I should have gone up to them in the welcoming line.* She looks at all the other middle-eastern guests, but no one is wearing glasses.

She wonders if it's a henchman in the tunnel, but the clothes were so exotic looking. Whoever it is must have money and be dressed up for the wedding. None of these guests feel like a mass murderer. She gives up. Right on cue, Friar Xavier materializes on the chair next to her. *"Any luck Bridget?"*

"Sorry Friar, wish I could pick him out of the crowd, but I can't. Maybe it's not precognition. Maybe my dream was just an ordinary, run of the mill nightmare."

Friar Xavier looks longingly at the plate of delectable food and suggests, *"Perhaps at the moment, you were only able to make out certain features. It is often that way at a moment of stress."*

"You're right. I read that victims of crimes have a very hard time giving descriptions of their assailant for that very reason. So it isn't just me."

"Pardon?"

"Ah. No problem. Thank you, Friar Xavier, you're the best. I was beginning to doubt my abilities, and it's just my human side working against me. I will let go of my physical description and look only with my 'inner eye' to really see the people around me."

"Then I will leave you to it. Good luck dear Bridget, God is with you."

She pushes her dinner plate away and takes a long drink of water. She walks into the lobby away from the music and noise and finds a quiet corner with a beautiful marble fountain. The sounds of running water and the beautiful plants help to ground her and remove any doubt in her ability to get the job done. She takes a few deep breaths and begins to gather her inner strength as Mick has taught her.

She walks back into the room and begins to check out people's auras. She narrows her focus down to one person at a time, and it takes a long time. She can see bright colors showing the enjoyment of the day and some dark shades of gray. Noticing nothing out of the ordinary, she turns her focus on the wedding party again. She is too late. They're no longer at their table.

She moves quickly to catch up with them and catches sight of a wraith at the corner of her eye. What's that? It's not friendly. She can't see anyone. Not a friendly spirit or fae. She has the feeling she is being watched. She can't call Mick or Que-tip. She hasn't seen anything solid or identifiable. Something is there and watching her. Then she catches a glimpse at an aura, so black with evil that the darkness has bled into the other rainbow colors, blocking any additional information she may have been able to gather.

So much darkness. Now she knows where the expression 'makes my skin crawl' comes from. *Are the nightmares coming at me during the day? Are they getting worse? Am I hallucinating?*

She snaps out of her stupor just in time to bump into a waiter and fall in the midst of a large tray of plates that he was carrying into the kitchen. Food is flying everywhere. Bridget watches in shock as a large plate of goose pate hits a woman wearing an enormous hat shaped like an orchid. Red wine makes its way to a woman in a pure white sari.

Bridget jumps up and bends to help pick up some of the plates but falls again as she bumps heads with a gorgeous guy. It's Mick. He looks right at home at this stuffy reception. More like a model with shoulder length sun-bleached hair curling in waves to his shoulders, and his deeply tanned distinctive face adds an elegant air about him that tells the world he was born of royal blood.

Mick puts his arm around her and helps her out to the lobby. There is nothing to worry about; Mick is strong she is safe. She turns to thank him, and her mouth won't work. He is looking at her with the most beautiful honey golden eyes and those long lashes that are to die for; laugh lines frame his eyes. What the...?

He's laughing at her! He's pointing at her and laughing. What a jerk, she pulls away from him and marches over to the elevator. She pushes the button to go down to the parking garage. The elevator doors open, and she gets a look at herself in the full-length mirror. Well, it doesn't look like a fancy creation shaped like an orchid but wearing a lobster in her hair did look original. She starts laughing and turns back to thank Mick. He's gone.

Chapter 19

Bridget's Apartment
Battersea, England

"Bridget, I think it's time for you to call in Scotland Yard."

"You're right Friar, but I don't know if they will believe me."

"I have never had them listen to me. I think I am on their records as a mental case. Otherwise, I would go in your place."

"Thank you Peter, but I know Charlie. I've helped him before, and I think he'll listen to me. Hopefully, he'll have enough pull to have the tunnels put under surveillance."

Mick is wearing jeans and a black t-shirt but still looks as handsome as he did at the party. Well except for the frown. "You have other matters on your plate right now. It is time to turn this over to the local law enforcement."

"I hate to find myself agreeing with flea-bite, but he is right. You must prepare for Morrigan's followers. I can read something new in your aura, Bridget. Have you had another encounter with the flame thrower from the tunnel?" asks a puzzled Que-tip.

Everyone starts talking at once.

"Calm down guys. I don't know what it is. Maybe it's stress causing the dark areas in my aura, Que-tip. Would dark spots show up if you are overly worried about something?"

"Added to the stress you are already under, I would say so."

Friar leaves his seat on her fireplace mantel and is now pacing the floor in step with Peter. Mick sits down next to her on the couch and is staring at her. Que-tip flies over and perches on the arm of the couch. They are all waiting for her to explain. *I guess they aren't buying my stress excuse.*

"Okay guys, yesterday at the reception, just seconds before the waiter bumped into me, I thought I saw something. A wraith, a spirit, something flashed by so quickly I couldn't make out what it was. I wouldn't be upset except that I sensed an evil blackness like I've never felt before."

"Are you certain that the feeling was coming from a creature and not from a human who was in the same area?"

"Dang it, Friar; I hadn't thought of that. Here I'm putting out feelers to read auras, and I received a hit at the same instant that I caught the movement, and I assumed that they both were connected. If the feeling of evil wasn't coming from whatever was watching me, then it must have come from a human source. The man I was after was there at the reception. I bet the older brother, Prince Oama, walked by me, and I didn't notice. We can't take any chances this late in the game. Que-tip, do you think that you could assign a faeire to watch Prince Oama and report his movements back to us?"

"Certainly," Qur-tip agrees, happy to have more assignment. Nods and in a shower of sparkles is off.

"What about the younger Prince?"

"I'm hoping that he'll be so busy with wedding plans and keeping his beautiful fiancée amused, he won't have time for anything else. If I'm reading this right, he and his bride and the Queen will be safe until the wedding day."

"You think that the older Prince will take out his brother?" Peter asks.

"Well, from what I've read, the young prince is gaining a lot of followers in their country. He could overthrow his brother and gain control. What a perfect opportunity for Prince Oama. He can remove a potential threat to his throne and turn the followers that are in favor of 'western ways' against England just by saying that the target was his brother and not the Queen."

Mick shakes his head. "Bridget, how do you think of such things?"

"I love to read, Mick. History is great. You learn about government being over-thrown by siblings."

"Interesting I thought perhaps you were reading Shakespeare." Mick frowns but Peter and the Friar laugh.

Bridget ignores them and says, "Someone told me that history keeps repeating itself. That everyone should learn history so that we can prevent the worst of it from happening again."

"What do you want me to do Bridget?"

"I hate to ask this of you Peter, but could you keep Michelle busy. They have not caught the dog-nappers yet, and she's a nervous wreck. Take her to the coast or something. There's nothing any of us can do at this point. I'm going to see Charlie and ask him to add surveillance cameras in the tunnels."

"Okay Bridget, you are right, it is better to keep busy. Call me anytime; I will not be too far away."

"Thank you, Peter, I'll call Charlie now and set up a meeting."

Chapter 20

East End
London, England

"Que-tip checks in with her faeire team on dognapper watch.

An excited Lynne reports, "I think the police are close to finding the criminals that took Queen Mum's dogs."

"Great news Lynne, are you still tagging along after that Inspector?"

"I don't let him out of my sight. I will let you know as soon as we have them in hand."

"Are you okay with leaving Willie on his own?"

"I have Kasondra and Natalie keeping an eye on him."

"Brilliant, keep at it." With a sparkle of color, Que-tip heads to the Foster Land Underground, to check on the tube watch.

She set the meeting for the little park across from the Scotland Yard building in the hopes the relaxing atmosphere would help. It didn't. Sitting on a bench in a small area of peace and calm in a fast moving area of the city. Bridget with Mick in dog form at her feet watched as Charlie explodes. He is red in the face when he shouts. "What are you thinking Bridget? There is no way I can get the blokes at the yard to go along with this. They will want to know who my informant is, run it up the chain of command and then it will go into committee. It will take weeks."

"We don't have weeks. My source tells me that this will take place within the next couple of days. What can we do?" Bridget pleads.

"Let me think about it. I will let you know. You do trust your source?"

"One hundred percent."

"I will get back to you."

"When Charlie? I must know if you will do something or not."

"If I say no, then what, you will set up surveillance yourself?"

"If I have to."

"Are there more at home like you?" he laughs, shakes his head and gets up to leave, bends over and pats Mick on the head, "nice dog."

"I'll 'nice dog' him." Growls Mick.

"Mick, he's just friendly, what's the matter?"

"It sounds as though you will get no help from that direction."

"You never know, Charlie may be able to do it."

She looks at the expression on Mick's dog face and laughs. *"Okay, let's think of what to do. What's plan 'B' if Charlie cannot set up surveillance in the tunnel?"*

"You were hoping that Charlie would set up electronic surveillance that would be monitored by a professional, round the clock, 24-hour security staff of the Exchange. I agree that is what is needed. I have it, call Miss Ear-Wax."

"Call Que-tip, why... Oh, I know, good thinking. You need to stop calling her ear wax; it really gets her mad."

"I know, that is why I do it," Mick says with a funny, lopsided, doggie grin.

Bridget shakes her head at Mick, *"Let's call her from the car so she can materialize without having to use energy to stay invisible."*

It will be nice to get away from this grass. I think I found a flea. Mick grumbles as Bridget laughs.

"Thanks for coming Que-tip. I'm not sure Charlie will be able to get the help we need on his own. He's a great guy, but he is new to the yard and doesn't have the clout to pull the strings we need to get this done in a hurry. Can you and the other 'communication' ladies get to work on all the members of the yard that Charlie reports to?"

"Piece of pie!" She squeaks and in a whirlwind of sparkling dust, Que-tip goes off to work her magic.

Bridget lets out a deep breath and lays her head back on the headrest. Mick, back in human form sits in the passenger seat.

She looks over and asks, "Mick, what else can I do? I helped Friar by finding a clue that helped to uncover the identity of the dog-nappers. I helped Peter to camouflage the tunnel entrance that leads under St. Paul's and set it up so the would-be terrorists would get caught attempting to blow up the Exchange. What do you think? Did I miss anything?"

Mick scratches his arm as he answers. "I do not believe so. Why, do you feel that there is something left undone?"

"I just need to get some sleep. Maybe what's nagging at the back of my mind will come to me when I dream. Just hope I wake up and remember what the answer is."

"You do not look as though you got much sleep," Mick says as Bridget walks into the kitchen the next morning.

"Thanks, I look that bad huh? I can't seem to get the feeling out of my head that I'm missing something."

She pours herself a cup of coffee and walks into the living room still trying to figure out what she missed. Mick helps himself to coffee and a muffin and follows.

As soon as Mick sits down, Bridget asks, "Let's start with the dog-nappers. Why? What would a pair of third-rate thieves hope to gain by stealing the Queen's dogs? They are not bright enough to plan it on their own. Someone must be familiar enough with Sandringham House to have known the layout."

"They must have wanted the attention of the world to be on the dog-napping. Why would you steal something that belongs to a wonderful lady who is loved by so many? What would you accomplish?" Mick asks.

"Do you know how many billions of people around the world love animals? If they do not have good feelings for the Queen, just remember the headlines and pictures of the cute puppies. Here you have a sweet old lady who loves animals, and someone is causing her pain by taking her loved ones away, and perhaps harming them. That news caused a great deal of emotion. How did you feel when you read the news?"

"You are right. Even I felt sad," Mick admits.

"Then you are not the average reader. Often when one reads something that causes so much emotion, it takes us to an even more evil place within, the desire for revenge. Some folks want the evil doers to suffer. Sometimes they have a preconceived notion of who the evildoers are and retaliate in small ways. Forwarding negative emails or commenting negatively on the World Wide Web. In this case, France is the focus as the evil doer behind the dog-napping. What is happening in France that world opinion would hurt?"

Before Mick can answer, Bridget jumps up. "Wait, I read something before all of this started. France wants to be the next home of the summer Olympics. They were number one in the standing and the decision was to be made next week."

"That could be it then. If world opinion is set against a country, the Olympic committee would never select them."

"We need to find out what country is now the number one choice to win the spot as the host of the next Summer Olympics. Wait, I'll Google it."

Bridget works her cell, finds what she wants, jumps up, shakes her head and plops back down.

"What did you find?"

"This is crazy; I can't believe it." A sad Bridget shakes her head in denial.

"What country is behind this mess?" Mick demands.

"Us! The United States of America is now at the top of the list. How could someone from my country do something so low?"

"We are .... I mean people are human, and humans, no matter where they live can be influenced by evil, if they allow themselves to be."

"I know. That is why I had to stop Morrigan from using the fae to influence people. To encourage evil acts."

"It sounds like her work. She must have set it in action before you defeated her."

Bridget bows her head and quietly says, "I don't understand. It must be some big corporate owner who is not satisfied with only making a few billion; he wants to make more. Why are folks so greedy? And don't tell me television; I have heard that one before."

"There is some proof that television does make people feel that they need more things to be happy. If they do not have the latest, must-have item, they feel deprived. Even at the highest level. Your average corporate leader is obsessed with the bottom line, in making more money. They seldom stop long enough to appreciate the blessings they already have."

"Charlie said that they are monitoring the bank accounts of the guys, they believe, took the dogs. They think one of them will come out of hiding long enough to pull the money from the bank account, and they can pinpoint an area to search. I'll let him know our theory and see if he was able to follow the money trail back to the person who paid them to do this. Do you think there is anything we can do to get France back in the running with the Olympic committee?"

Mick shakes his head. "Sorry, my girl. That is the power of negative thinking. It takes a great deal of good to overcome the smallest seed of ill feelings, whether against a person or a country."

"So when people hear that an American was behind this hideous crime, they will not just blame that one person. World opinion will be against all of us and not just the idiot who did it."

"I'm afraid so; it is always the case. Remember your history." Mick takes a sip of his coffee. No longer hungry for the muffin.

"I love talking things over with you but sometimes talking with you is depressing. I'm going to call Charlie to fill him in and see if he has any news for us. Then I'm going to have another cup of coffee and call Michelle and talk about fun stuff."

Chapter 21

**East End
London, England**

Lynne sits on the brim of Charlie's hat as he waits in a van parked on Oak Street. She telepathically asks, "Cade, are they still inside?"

"Yes, they are arguing as usual. It is hard work getting these guys quiet enough to plant any suggestions."

"Charlie and his team are in place. Let me know when to nudge him along."

"Right On."

Many more minutes pass before Lynne hears from Cade. "Okay Lynne, David and I finally got through to them. They are leaving for the pub now."

Charlie is texting. Lynne flies down to his ear and whispers. "Look out the window! Now!"

Charlie alert now looks out at the two dog-nappers and says, "Those are our guys. Brad, you, and Steve follow them.

We will go inside and make sure the dogs are here before we make our arrest."

Lynne can't wait for Charlie's report; she asks, "Cade, how are the puppies?"

"Sleeping, but not natural like, I bet the bloody goons used a drug to knock them out.

"I checked they are all alive," David reports.

"Thank you, fellows, I will make sure that Charlie calls Bridget right off."

"Great news guys, that was Charlie on the phone, they got the guys who took the puppies. Best of all, the puppies are all okay. Evidence proves that the dogs were given ether, to put them to sleep. They recovered from that. The only problem now is that they have the run of the palace, and the Queen is having so much fun playing with them that nothing else is getting done."

The small front room fills with sparklers as Que-tip twirls and the Friar dances around with her. Peter is laughing at the strange sight of Que-tip dancing. He was just getting used to Mick changing to human form. Bridget says he may be able to see spirits someday; he hopes she's right.

Mick comes over to Bridget and says, "Good job my girl; you have made many, many people happy today. You are very good at this detecting business."

Bridget laughs and hugs him tight. "Time to celebrate! How about tea and cookies or I may have some leftovers, we could make some sandwiches?"

Peter jumps up from his seat on the couch. "My treat Bridge, I will just pop over to the fish and chips stand and get us all a proper meal."

"Sounds great to me," Bridget looks around at her new family of friends and suggests, "Better get some extras, maybe a hamburger or two and a milkshake."

Que-tip twirls and yelling, "Yippee," bumps into the television set. Bridget runs to make sure she is okay only to see a flash as she dances past. *I think I better watch her sugar intake.*

While they eat supper, they watch an old rerun of 'Upstairs, Downstairs.' Bridget looks over at Que-tip, she is lying on Peter's shoulder, and they are both asleep. The Friar is watching everything on TV, especially the commercials, they are his favorite. His latest game is trying to figure out what the advertiser is trying to sell. He very seldom figures it out, but when he does, he dances around for a while and then settles down to watch some more. Mick is also asleep with his head on her shoulder. It feels good just to relax. She lays her head back against the couch.

She is back in the tunnel. *A scream echoes thru the tunnel, a cry that comes from the very heart of a nightmare. It reverberates for a long moment and then deadly silence.*

"Bridget wake up, please wake up, it is only a dream."

She opens her eyes. Mick is standing over her, nose to nose. "I'm okay Mick it's only a dream."

She looks into his beautiful eyes, so filled with concern for her. She feels a strange pull in the vicinity of her chest, like a vise gripping her heart. She loves Mick. She doesn't know how she will ever survive without him. She starts to tear up.

An anxious Peter asks, "What's going on, are you okay Bridget?"

"I'm fine Peter, honest." She looks around at Friar Xavier and Que-tip, I'm okay guys. It was just another scary dream."

"What was it about, it may be important," Mick asks.

"I don't think so; guys let's have a cup of tea and plan what we are going to do tomorrow. What time should we be at the Cathedral?"

"Half eight," an anxious Friar Xavier answers.

"Okay, I'll be there at eight-thirty, the service starts at ten. Will I have any problem getting into the main chapel that early?"

"I am not certain what security measures are in place. Have you heard from your friend at the yard?" Peter asks.

"Sorry guys, I was so excited about the puppies that I totally forgot the other great news. Charlie, with a lot of help from our fae friends..." she winks at Que-tip, "was able to get some very high-tech surveillance equipment that will alert them to any entry under the Exchange."

"The buggers may be looking for such equipment and be prepared to dismantle it."

"You're right Peter, they thought of that. They want them to think that the tech alarm is the only one. They also installed trip wires."

"Tripwires? What's that?" A puzzled Que-tip asks.

"It's an old-fashioned set-up Que-tip, not something these guys will be expecting. Sometimes they are connected to a bomb that goes off when the wire is triggered. In this case, the wires are connected to an alarm that sounds above ground in the security office. It's the best they can do for a backup plan."

"Where do you want me?"

"Peter, we know that the Royals are also a target. The Queen and her family are well protected. I am not sure about the bride-to-be. If you could just stroll by the home of Lady Margaret and see if you sense anything off, you know what I mean?"

"Excellent, should I meet up with you in the American Chapel?"

Bridget nods. "Yes, if you can, you may not be able to get through the crowd. I'll text you my whereabouts, be sure to keep your mobile on."

"I will; I like having it handy," Peter admits.

"Friar, you, of course, will be next to the Queen. Que-tip, could you and your team go in early and check the area for anything that does not feel right. The Queen's security will check for bombs as a normal routine for any place she may be, but we may be wrong about the tunnel, or they may have changed their minds and will use another means."

Mick crosses his arms and announces, "I will stay with you."

"Sorry Mick, you can't stay with me. I want to go into the Cathedral myself. It will be easier to hide one person."

"I will cloak and accompany you," Mick insists.

"You can wait just outside the door. I will be fine. Security will be checking for bombs inside the Cathedral and we know that we have the tunnels covered. I will be fine; I need to check that every angle is covered." Mick does not look happy.

"Please Mick, don't worry so much. You'll get wrinkles and wind up looking like a Blood Hound." She laughs at his expression.

Chapter 22

St. Paul's Cathedral
London, England

Eight-thirty is way too early to be up and about on a Saturday morning, but St. Paul's is packed with people. At least a hundred of them are walking about taking pictures or doing last minute tasks.

The main part of the cathedral sits under a high domed ceiling, and Bridget stands in awe at its great size. The large open space must be able to seat at least a thousand people.

The floor of the cathedral, tiled in a black and white checkerboard pattern is a brilliant backdrop for the red roses women are placing, in small bouquets, to the end of each aisle.

Everywhere she looks there are flower arrangements. Large bundles of white carnations, lilies, and roses. Added into all that white are deep, dark, red roses, which stand out to make a dramatic statement.

Wish they didn't remind her of blood spilled on a wedding gown.

She passes a woman who looks like a wedding planner. She is dressed in a dark red silk dress with a matching red and white short jacket, standing with several guys in tuxes. *Talk about color coordinating; even her clipboard is red.*

Bridget walks down the narrow hallway between the pillars looking, for what, she doesn't know. She wishes her Sherlock sense would kick in soon. She knows that something is not right, but she still has no idea what's missing.

Up ahead is the 'Great Circle' under the dome. She can see the choir gathered for a final practice. A few hundred steps above her head, she can make out men in uniform making the rounds of the three circular galleries that make up the inside of the dome, their reports to each other echoing off the walls in scary sounding whispers.

She ducks behind one of the pillars when she spots one of the Queen's guards setting up gold rope barricades, and asking tourists to move on. He is explaining that this section is being closed off due to the upcoming wedding. Of course, this just excites folks, and they stay around taking pictures. Many look like they are ready to camp out and wait to see the Queen. Bridget wonders how that will work for them. She wanders around, keeping out of sight of the guard. The choir begins singing a hymn.

The wedding planner walks by with her entourage, "The bridal party will then move to the Ambulatory to sign the Registers." She stops, looks at Bridget, decides she is not important to the wedding and continues walking. *Well, that felt weird.*

Bridget is ready to give up; her spidery sensors are not working. She sits down in a pew and says a quick prayer for guidance. As she bends her head, she spots a colorful brochure lying on the floor. She picks it up and reads the cover, 'The Insider's Guide to St. Paul's.' She opens to the first page and reads, 'Within the cathedral are plaques, carvings, monuments, and statues dedicated to a wide range of people. The bulk is related to the British military with several lists of servicemen who died in action - the most recent being the Gulf War. There are special monuments to Admiral Nelson and the Duke of Wellington, on horseback, unveiled in 1912. Be sure to visit our famous Crypt.' *Crypt that sounds spooky.*

She continues reading. 'Entrances to the downstairs crypt are in both transepts, on either side of the dome. St. Paul's substantial cathedral crypt contains over 200 memorials as well as another chapel and the treasury. Many notable figures are buried in St. Paul's Cathedral crypt, such as Florence Nightingale and Lord Nelson.

'The Treasury has very few treasures. Many were lost over the years. It is unknown how the thieves gained entry through the crypt. Some speculate that it was by means of a secret passage used in 1810 when a major robbery took almost all of the remaining precious artifacts, its location remains a mystery to this very day.'

OH no! There can't be another way in that we don't know.

Maybe it's another entrance to the Underground tunnel. Bridget runs the length of the long hallway to the back of the main floor. At the east end of the

Cathedral, behind the High Altar, is the American Memorial Chapel. To the right of that are stairs she noticed on her last visit.

She continues to move quickly while trying not to draw the attention of the guards. She looks again at the Choir and Altar and gets a tightening in her chest of the history and beauty destroyed if she doesn't stop this.

She finally reaches the stairs and finds a large red velvet cord blocking the entrance to the stone steps leading down to the lower floors. 'No Entrance without prior approval! Visitors must be accompanied by a church guide.'

No way, Jose! No time! Bridget lifts up her Dolce Cabana pencil skirt, exposing more skin than should be shown in these halls, and steps over the rope. The stone steps, worn in the center, are totally uneven. She almost takes a header down the entire flight and grabs the railing. She removes her shoes and continues down what must be equal to two long flights of steps. *I really must remember to donate some money to this place; they seriously need more lights down here.*

She walks down the hallway to a vaulted room, labeled 'Nelson's Chamber.' She looks in and sees a black sarcophagus, but no door. She continues down the hallway to another room. She sees a simple casket made of granite with the name Arthur Wellington. *Wow, I have to come back and check that out later. That's the Duke.*

After minutes that seem like hours of running around in circles, she stands under a dimly lit light bulb and checks the brochure to see if she has missed something. *Where the heck is the Treasury?*

She reads, 'The crypt of St. Paul's is the largest in Western Europe, and unusual for a cathedral, it is the exact 'footprint' of the cathedral floor.'

No wonder she can't find this place. *Okay, think,* the Choir was the first part of the cathedral to be built. If the Treasury of artifacts were here, it would be in the oldest part of the building. As with most churches, built during the same time as this one, it's shaped like a cross.

She retraces her steps to the center of the crypt and goes from the west side of the building to the east side and then she finds the less elaborate tombs and the room dedicated to the Treasury.

Of course, it has a door and of course, it's locked! The old fashioned lock has not been open for a long time, *now what?* A credit card won't work to open that. *What if alarms go off if I open it?* Bridget takes a deep breath and reasons, if the lock has not been opened, then no one else has gone in. Maybe the door is elsewhere?

She walks over to a light and checks the brochure again. She read something important, but what? She knows she was given the brochure for a reason, but what? *Come on Bridget think, where is the other entrance to the tunnels?*

"Bridget, it is half-nine, where are you?"

"Mick, I can't explain now but please go to the underground, directly beneath the Cathedral and see if you can find another opening?"

"Where are you?"

"I'm in the crypt under the choir area. The crypt is below street level about equal with the underground tunnel. I just read that there was a break-in here in 1810. I am looking for another opening to the

tunnel. *If there is one it may have explosives and our camouflage trick in the tunnel won't work. Please hurry!"*

"I am not going anywhere without you. You must leave the Cathedral now! Peter has had no word from Charlie that the culprits were captured, have you heard from him? The explosives may go off at any moment. Transport out of there!"

"I have time. The terrorists will wait until the service is underway and all the guests are here. I think I have about an hour. Is the Queen here?"

"No, but I have seen Prince Ammed and his older brother enter as well as their entourage. There are not many people from the Prince's country. I have seen only a handful, and they look like bodyguards. There are many famous people here getting their picture taken with the young Prince and sitting on the groom's side of the church. He is very popular with the young stars. It's like a who's who of Hollywood is here today."

"Please get word to Que-tip to make sure the fae keep an eye on the older brother. We need to know the second that he gets up to leave. Then we will know the

bombs are ready to go off. If we have not heard from Charlie by then, we will need to start a fire or something to evacuate the church in a hurry. While he's still sitting there, we are safe!"

"Okay, I am in the tunnel now. I will find the other entrance if there is one."

"Thank you, Mick! You're great!"

Bridget takes a deep breath and closes her eyes. *Where is it?* She clears her mind and 'stops the constant chatter' as Mick has taught her. Breathe deep and let go. Breathe deep and let go. She sees an image. She is on the train, and Florence is telling her that the French are wary of people that smile too much.

Florence! That's it! The brochure says that Florence Nightingale's buried here. *Where?* She runs along the hallway looking into all the rooms. *Why is this place so huge, I will never find it in time!* Bridget runs past one room after another.

What is that? She stops and backs up. An old fashioned kerosene lamp sits on top of a stone tomb. *That must be her; she would visit soldiers at night, on the battlefield, she is, 'The lady of the lamp.'*

Bridget wishes she had a lamp right now. The room allocated to Florence Nightingale is dim, illuminated only by the low wattage lamp in the hall. *Where is that door? Yoo-hoo! Florence, are you here? I could use your help! Florence, please come out, come out, wherever you are?* Bridget twirls around looking for her to appear. She is disappointed when she doesn't get an answer.

Maybe it's a secret passage? Bridget gets on her knees and looks under the tomb to check for loose stones and sees a light. The light is in the shape of a beam given off by a pen light and is coming closer. Dang the security guards would check now. Maybe they will keep walking down the hallway and not come into this room. *How do I talk my way out of this? Maybe he will keep making rounds, and I can slip out?*

Bridget stays on her knees, and the light comes into the room. *Not good!*

She can see the hand holding the light; the sleeve looks familiar. A bright red satin trimmed with gold braid on the cuff and exotic designs sewed into the fabric with gold thread. *The Prince!*

"Bridget, are you okay, where are you?"

"No Mick I'm not okay, I need help. I'm kneeling behind Florence Nightingale's tomb. This floor's cold. The Prince is here. He can't see me. I think he will be heading your way. He's walking to the end of the far wall. He's looking at a display from the Crimean War. Where the elaborate display ends, there's a wall, paneled in what looks like the original wood that built this place. He's raising his left hand and is putting it on a single panel above his head. With the other hand, he put the penlight in his mouth and is now pressing another panel at waist height. Great, it's opening! Can you see it from where you are?"

"No, no movement at all."

"I don't think he's carrying anything. Could bombs be small enough to put in a pocket?"

"Bridget get out of there now!"

"I will, I promise. Keep looking for him!"

"Of course, but you must promise me to leave the building now!"

"I will, I promise, don't you believe me?"

"I do, now get a move on!"

"Okay, bye, be careful, he may have a gun."

Bridget decides to leave as soon as Prince Oama is in the passage. She plans to follow him and leave the church as Mick demanded. She didn't lie to Mick. She is leaving the church the same way the Prince is. There is no way she could leave him. She has to stop him. The panel is starting to close; she drops her shoes and runs after him. Using both hands to keep the panel open, she steps into a wooden structure that's creaking with her every move.

Chapter 23

Foster Lane Station
Underground Tunnel

Alan telepathically calls out, "Sam; they are coming your way. We are in luck, no Morrigan followers in sight. They must believe their job is done so they are off to find new people to harm."

"I got the one in front; you take the guy following," Sam responds.

Cade instructs David, "Be sure to keep his attention away from the trip wires. We want these blokes caught up tight as can be."

"Right On," David responds and is off in a flash.

"Ladies, are you all set to make sure the guards are ready to get to work?" Cade asks.

"Sure thing Cade, Natalie and I have them covered."

"Thanks, Leonda, how about you Lynne, are you still with Charlie?"

"I have him. I may have to turn off the computer to get his attention, but he will be there."

Prince Oama is making noise as he confidently walks to the underground tunnel to check on his men. Bridget lets the door close slowly behind her, and tries not to cough on the dust and dirt that the Prince has stirred up. She hurries after him and his barely visible beam of light. If she loses him now, she will scream.

She doesn't want to think of what this dirt is doing to her new outfit. Her nylons are toast. *Ouch, what am I walking on... thank goodness I don't have a light. I really don't want to know.*

Her cell phone starts blasting the Star Spangled Banner, Michelle's idea of a joke when she programmed her ring tone. Bridget gasps aloud and jumps back a couple of steps to the wall. She immediately bites down on her lip as she hurries to shut her cell phone off. She gets it out of her pocket and sees a text from Charlie, it reads, 'Terrorists and explosives in custody, call later.' For a brief moment, she's so happy; she can't wait to tell everyone. Then she's alert to a deadly silence. She hears no retreating footsteps and sees no light. With the primitive instinct of the hunted, she knows he's out there, waiting for her. He heard her cell.

She listens to the now silent room and telepathically cries out, *"Mick I'm in a room under the crypt. There must be a way out of here into the tunnel. I got word that we're not going to be blown up, but Prince Oama knows that I followed him, and is now waiting for me. I'm trapped. If I move, and try to go back up to the crypt, he'll hear me. What should I do?"*

"Transport out now!"

"I can't, I'm so scared, I can't concentrate."

"Stay where you are, I am coming to get you."

"Please don't, he has a gun!"

She feels her way forward, hoping to get to the darkest side of the room, away from any sudden light. She moves, but not fast enough. The light hits her face.

"Who are you? Ah, the clumsy lady from the reception. Are you a reporter? No matter, there is nothing to report."

Bridget screams, but it is the kind of scream she had in her nightmares, a choked soundless cry that reaches no one. She turns to run and uses her mind to create a shell around her for protection. Fear stifles her first attempt and before she can make another a lacerating pain slices her in two. The force of the bullet knocks her to the ground. Her heart is racing with fear and pain she yells out, *"I love you, Mick, I'm sorry. I messed up."*

She feels Mick materialize beside her and hears, "Huff. Stay with her."

She can feel Mick's arms around her. Moments later she hears the blood-curdling scream she'd heard in her nightmare and opens her eyes.

"Mick, is everything okay?"

"All is fine now, how are you?"

"I think I may have passed out. I have an unfortunate tendency to freak myself out at the worst possible moments."

She looks down at her beautiful new outfit covered in blood.

"I'm okay if I don't look at the blood." *That's my blood, yuck. I can do this, or pass out again, whichever comes first.*

Mick taught her to protect herself with a shell or heal herself whichever was needed. She will relax; *okay breathe... Ouch! Okay, not too deeply.*

She feels lightheaded and woozy. She looks at her arm and examines the wound. She somehow knows the bullet has passed through and nothing vital is damaged. She has to stop the bleeding. She goes to work with her mind to close the exit wound. She then concentrates on closing the entrance wound. With that done she gives herself permission to pass out.

Chapter 24

Bridget's Apartment
Battersea, England

Bridget wakes up, just where she wants to be, at home in Battersea, in her own bed. She won't even question how she got clean and into her PJ's. She feels good, but boy does she have to use the bathroom. She opens her eyes and sees that she has a room full of visitors.

"Ah, guys, can this wait a bit. I would like a little privacy for now."

No one moves. Finally, Michelle comes over, and without looking around says, "Peter, please take Mick into the front parlor, we will join you there soon."

She smiles at a calm and efficient Michelle, she is in full caring mode, treating Bridget, like a puppy needing medical attention. It feels a little strange, but as long as Michelle helps her to the bathroom, she is fine with strange.

If Michelle had seen what Bridget saw when she opened her eyes, she would really freak out. Crammed into her small bedroom, is her entire Irish family and new English friends: Que-tip, David, Alan, Cade, Deirdre, Regan, Natalie, Ana, Kasondra, Samantha, Leonda, and a dozen other faeire.

Friar Xavier has also brought a friend she recognized as Florence; she's sitting on the bed, looking very concerned. A Nurse is a nurse forever. Bridget leans on both Michelle and Florence as she makes her way to the bathroom. *Being injured is really getting to be a pain. I've got to get my magic good enough to stop getting hurt.* When she sits down, she still has no privacy.

Michelle, puzzled, states the obvious. "You have no fever now. Your skin feels cool to the touch."

"I...ah must be a fast healer," Bridget mumbles. Little did Michelle know that leaning on a ghost would bring down anyone's fever, it's like being immersed in a bathtub filled with ice.

After a lot of fussing by both of her caregivers, Bridget is allowed to sit up in the front parlor. Peter has made a pot of tea and brought more cupcakes. She is feeling a little dizzy. After the room came back into focus, she asks, "How are the dogs doing?"

"The Dorgis are all showing a little sign of being malnourished, but there are no ill effects of the ether that the villains used to keep them quiet. I hope they keep those monsters in a kennel for life!"

"Hey, it's great to see your French attitude showing. I wouldn't want you angry at me. Good thing your 'villains' are safe behind bars," says Peter. He's looking at Michelle with more than just laughter in his eyes.

"Peter, did you fill Michelle in on what happened at the church?" Bridget asks.

"Yes, I did. She thought that you were very brave to follow the Prince to get an autograph for her."

"You Americans are Hollywood crazy. Why would a crowd of people want an autograph from the Prince? Imagine having a crowd of people knocks you down a flight of stairs. All of that pushing and shoving for an autograph, crazy. He is in all the papers; you should see."

Bridget quickly scans the headlines:

The Times, 'Queen Faces Empty Altar!'

The Sun, 'Lady Gets Cold Feet.'

The Telegraph reports, "Prince Oama pleads no comment' on the question of hurt feelings of his younger brother."

"What! Oh no! I thought Prince Oama would be in jail...."

Bridget looks over at Florence and remembers their discussion on the train, *'Someone who smiles all the time is not to be trusted.'*

"You were not talking just about the French, were you?" She asks Florence.

Florence gives her a slight smile and waves goodbye. Bridget looks at Mick, and all of the fae gathered.

For Michelle's sake, she holds up the papers and pretends that she is reading and asks, *"It was Prince Ammed in the crypt? How could I have been so wrong?"*

Que-tip answers, *"It was him alright. It seems he had a brilliant plan to remove his brother from his rightful place next in line to the throne and place the blame on England. He would appear from the rubble as a survivor and begin to assist in the rescue* mission. He had it all planned. Mick was able to read his thoughts when Daniel met up with him in the tunnel."

Bridget asks, "Why isn't the real story in the papers?"

Que-tip puts her hands on her waist and says in disgust, "Politics. Our government is honoring Prince Oama's request, and Lady Chaternning's family is being paid quite handsomely to take the blame for backing out of the wedding. The only knowledge the public will have of any of this is that the Lady left Prince Ammed waiting at the altar."

"Is Prince Ammed in jail in his own country?"

"Not exactly, it seems he had a bit of fright. Something he saw in the tunnel has affected his mind. When Charlie found him, he was lying in the fetal position, babbling about fire breathing dragons. He will be in a mental facility for the rest of his life."

"Daniel was in the tunnel? My Red Dragon of Wales friend?"

Bridget looks at Mick and asks, "How did that happen?"

"He wanted to help, and I suggested he stood guard when I went to check on you.

Of course, he had to see for himself that you were okay. Then he showed himself to Ammed. He enjoyed himself."

"How did Prince Ammed know of the secret passage in the crypt?"

"It seems one of his former classmates got drunk one night and bragged about his ancestor robbing the treasury and made the mistake of showing Prince Ammed. They found his skeleton in the passageway."

"OMG, that guy was pure evil."

"That is why his parents sent him away to school. They hoped to keep his insanity hidden from his fellow countryman."

"What about the guys that they caught with the explosives?"

"They are local hires, same as the guys they arrested for snatching the dogs. The Yard knows they were paid by an outside source but cannot trace the money back to the source. Both crimes will go on the books as solved and that makes the public happy."

"Who was behind the dog-napping?"

"We will never know for certain."

Bridget looks around the room. *"Thank you all so very much. Without your help, this would have been a major disaster."*

David flies over to her and kneels on the paper. *"A thousand pardons my lady. We were there to protect you. We have all been very anxious to hear that you have prevailed. We are a sorry lot to allow you to be injured."*

"David, you were all doing what I asked of you. I have learned that I must discover my gifts myself. I could have prevented my injury if I had kept calm and followed my teachings. This incident has shown me that I must be calm when I come up against all evil. For only with inner strength will I overcome all that is in store for me."

Bridget looks at all the fae gathered. *"I will be in touch soon, for I know now that I will continue fighting evil, and will need you all by my side."*

They all twirl and amidst a rainbow of color, leave. The room suddenly looks dull and drab without all of their wonderful, sparkling colors.

"Bridgette, you are very quiet. Are you feeling well?"

"I'm fine, Michelle, just tired. I think I'll go back to bed. I'm not feeling any pain. Just a little stiff but mostly tired. I wonder if this is what firefighters and law enforcement officer's face, extreme high shots of adrenalin and then the drop, the all over sense of exhaustion. I just need some sleep, don't worry."

Bridget wakes to daylight coming in the window. She hears excited voices and then realizes that it is Michelle and Peter, *why are they here?* They are very happy about something. She gets up, grabs her old robe and opens the door just in time to witness Peter and Michelle kiss. She is closing the door to give them some privacy when she looks down and sees Mick with his paws over his eyes and laughs out loud.

"Ah, *Oui*, you are awake. We have such news for you. Come sit with us."

"What's up with you guys, you look so happy."

Peter is waving a cream colored, heavily embossed envelope in the air. He waits until Bridget sits and then hands her an invitation, "Lord Chamberlain has been commanded by Her Majesty to invite you to the Investiture of Peter Kerins..."

"Wow fancy, what does it mean?"

"I don't know how to thank you, Bridget. Charlie told the Queen that I was responsible for saving St. Paul's and I am to be knighted. It will only be an honorary Knighthood, but I will be able to use Sir Peter Kerins on my business cards from now on," he bends his knee and gives a courtly bow that has them all laughing.

Peter sits down beside Bridget and takes her hand; he whispers, "You are not angry? You should be the one honored. You are the one that took all of the risks."

"Nonsense, you're the one that told me of the vision. You're the one responsible for saving the life of the Queen. Not me."

Bridget is embarrassed and knows she is starting to blush. Wanting to change the subject quickly she asks, "Michelle, what are you reading?"

"The invitation packet. It also contains all the information we require: dress codes, arrivals, and departures, parking, etc."

"What are you going to do?" Bridget asks Peter.

"Good form dictates that one always accepts," he replies.

"I know that you goof, of course, you will. Write to her majesty right away. That's so great. I'm so proud of you. Wow, my cousin will be an honorary Knight."

"You, Michelle and Charlie will be there to witness it."

Bridget shakes her head, "No way guys!"

Michelle reads, "The form of an investiture has remained the same since 1910. Each recipient is entitled to invite three guests to accompany them on their special day."

"Did you tell Charlie?" Bridget asks.

"Of course, I owe Charlie a great deal."

"Bridget, this is life changing, you must attend. It will surely be a boost to my business. I may have so many paying clients that I will be able to afford to make a permanent change in my home life." The last he said looking lovingly at Michelle.

And perhaps take on a business partner? Bridget thinks, unaware that Mick is listening to her thoughts.

Bridget looks over at a blushing Michelle. Resigned she asks, "What will we wear?"

Michelle shakes her head, "I am reading the pages that came with the invitation. I am surprised to see how traditional the British Court still is. No other institution could, in this modern age, still consider recommending that 'women wear hats' and advising that men wear 'morning dress or uniform.' White gloves are still the form, and I bet that they will stay immaculately clean as they glide along banisters, shake proffered royal hands, and wave goodbye in the ever-familiar royal manner."

"Well, I guess we don't have to worry about spreading germs," Bridget laughs.

A nervous Peter explains, "This is not a normal investiture. Those papers are for the traditional ceremonies. The ball will be held in my honor but not publically announced since we need to keep the reason secret. The ball will be the birthday of a royal family member. Normally an investiture is a daytime affair. The Queen does not wish to announce anything that had to do with the plan to destroy the Cathedral."

"Peter..." Bridget warns, looking at Michelle.

"Don't worry Bridget, I have told Michelle everything about myself. She is not concerned with my gift; she does not think I'm a freak. I had to tell her all about the Prince and the Cathedral."

Michelle jumps up from her chair and sits beside Peter on the couch and holds his hand, "No, No, it is a special gift to help others. Not a bad thing. If it were not for your 'feelings' the Queen would be no longer."

Bridget looks at Mick, "We are all going to a ball?"

A proud Peter beams. "Yes, you will be escorted by Charlie and I will, of course, escort Michelle."

"How will you be crowned?" Bridget asks. She is delighted to see him looking so happy and carefree.

Peter laughs, "I will be dubbed, as I am sure that you have seen in the movies."

"They really do that with a sword?" Bridget asks.

"Yes!"

"That is so cool." She looks at Michelle, "What do we do?"

Michelle hands the pages to Peter, "It is too much."

Peter laughs and reads from the pages of instructions. "We will all arrive at The Palace an hour early. We will then be conducted to the State Ball Room where we will be rehearsed in the procedure for being presented to the Queen.

"Then we all stand when the Queen enters the Ball Room, and we remain standing. The Lord Chamberlain then begins the ceremony proper by announcing the category of the honor. He then reads out my name and a brief explanation of why I am being honored.

"The only break from the form is that I will be the only recipient, rather than the customary much larger group. Only her guests and those in a position of security of the Queen and country will be present," Peter explains.

"So you kneel before the Queen, and she says "Arise Sir Knight......" Bridget laughs.

Peter blushes. "No, that is a complete fiction, although it does sound wonderful."

"Darn, I will miss most of the posh and circumstances," Bridget kids him.

"It will still be an experience we will never forget." Michelle giggles.

Peter tears his eyes away from Michelle and turns to Bridget. "Before I forget, Charlie wants you to call him as soon as you are feeling up to company. He would like to come to visit."

"First, I really need a shower and something to eat; I'm starving." Bridget heads to her bedroom.

Chapter 25

Bridget's Apartment
Battersea, England

They continue talking while they eat Michelle's version of grilled cheese sandwiches. Bridget never heard of grilled cheese made with white cheese? She doesn't know what kind it is, but it tastes great.

Bridget feels like a new person, clean, rested and her belly full. All is well with the world. She leans over to give Mick a bite of her sandwich, but he isn't at his usual place next to her. He isn't even in the dining room.

"Hey Mick, are you hungry, do you want a bite of my sandwich?"

No answer.

"Hey guys, did you see Mick?"

Michelle takes her eyes away from Peter long enough to answer. "I saw him out back when I was making the sandwiches. Don't worry. He may be just lazing around in the sun."

Maybe now that the crisis is over Mick went back to his real home. I guess he only likes to hang around when I need him. No longer hungry, Bridget pushes the sandwich away and announces that she is going for a walk.

Michelle looks her way and nods. "Hurry back; we have to practice making our obeisance."

"I'll be back soon." She wonders what the heck obeisance is, maybe purple cheese sandwiches. She checks the back yard again before she leaves. As she suspected, it's empty. No Mick.

She only walks a block when she hears, "Why so glum, chum?"

"Hi Que-tip, I thought you were off playing with your mates?"

"I did that; everyone's resting now." She flutters in front of Bridget until she moves her hair so Que-tip can sit on her shoulder. "I have one question, and then I'm off."

"Just one?" Bridget laughs.

"Why can't Mick take human form around Michelle?"

"It's complicated."

"So?"

Bridget can feel Que-tip tapping her foot on her shoulder and tries to explain. "If the world sees Mick, then I have to explain why we are always together. If Michelle marries Peter and we all grow old together, Mick will stay young; he will always be twenty."

They walk along in silence. Bridget is happy Que-tip isn't bugging her with more questions. She has no answers just major questions of her own, like what the heck does she do now?

Her latest nightmares are gone. In their place is an image of her walking along a dirt road on a cold and windy day. Maybe she gets to goof off until fall. Would Morrigan's Followers give her a couple of months to get a plan in place to get rid of all of them at once? She doubts it, but she just doesn't know what to do next.

She needs Mick; he's the one she likes to bounce her ideas off. She will give him some free time. He must be very tired teaching her. She hopes he isn't too mad at her. She did leave the Cathedral, just not the way he thought she would. Funny how much she misses him when he isn't around. The rest of her friends and family are just not the same. When he's near, she feels safe, no, not just safe. She feels as if she is someone special.

With most people, she always feels that whatever she does she will not measure up. With Mick, she feels as if she is accepted, just as she is, with all of her faults. He will be back soon. He wouldn't leave her now, would he?

Of course, she did make the decision to leave him. She has to go before he realizes how she feels about him. She shakes her head when she realizes that she is back at the apartment.

Bridget opens the front door to a madhouse. Charlie has arrived and is talking with Peter and Michelle as to what to expect at the Palace. There are a dozen or so faeire ladies fluttering around the room. They are so excited that the small front parlor looks like a rainbow erupted.

Tired from her walk, she tries to slip in quietly and head to the peace and quiet of her room.

"Brigitte, I am so happy you are here. We must practice our obeisance."

"Our what?"

"Our obeisance, it is most simple. It involves a curtsey to the Queen."

Bridget is in panic mode. She almost packs her bags to head back to Brooklyn. She thinks of a way out and suggests, "Back home we don't even curtsey to the First Lady. Can I just nod?"

"Good Morning Bridget, how are you feeling?" Charlie asks.

"I'm fine, just tired. Can't I just bow my head?"

"Men are blessed with having only to bow, a most simple act. A correct bow involves only a deep nod," Charlie informs them as he gives an example.

Peter looks as if he is in a state of panic. "Out of respect, it is expected that ladies will curtsey. If that is not comfortable, since you are not an English citizen, we will understand," sighs Peter.

How can he put so much guilt into a sigh? Still trying to get out of looking foolish, Bridget tries again. "Can I just bow from the waist?"

"Bridgette obeisance is so easy, you and I will practice. We will do it. We will do it for you, Peter, and for the fact that we respect your Queen."

Okay, I'm stuck now, just great.

Charlie, who had already received an honor for his help in locating the missing dogs, continues his instructions. "Once you have been presented, you are faced with the question of what to say. The Queen is always addressed as Your Majesty on the first count and after that as "Ma'am, this should rhyme with jam, not palm. Other members of the royal family will be treated with similar respect: Your Royal Highness then Sir or Ma'am.

"You should let the royal personage lead the conversation, not try to change the subject, and ask only the politest of questions. Is Your Majesty enjoying the performance?" is acceptable, but How's Philip and Charles? Is most definitely, absolutely out of the question. When you are in conversation with a member of the royal family, be yourself but remember that Her Royal Highness is not going to appreciate your company if it is too loud, tongue-tied, rude, or bumptious."

What the heck is bumptious? I'm sure he was looking at me when he said that. I know, I can play the... 'I'm not feeling too good card.' That's it; I will just play sick and not go.

Bridget looks at the excited faeire trying to get her attention and says to her human company, "Excuse me, guys. I'm a little worn out from my walk. I'll take a quick nap and join you guys later for dinner. Will that be okay?"

Michelle jumps up and hugs her. "Pardon, Brigitte. We are thoughtless. We will speak quietly. You rest and don't worry about dinner. We will get 'take away' and wake you later on when it is all set to dine."

The faeire follow Bridget into the bedroom. "You are not going to back out, Bridget. We are all here to help you."

"Que-tip, you really must stop listening to my thoughts, it is not polite."

The faeire ladies look subdued, and Bridget tries to explain, "Thank you, ladies, for your offer to help. I really appreciate it but, all I can think of is the movies I've watched where lines of young women parade before the Queen like vestal virgins adorned in white with feathers, trains, and fans to make their deep, and well-practiced curtseys. I will look like a fool, and I have nothing to wear."

With that Regan, Natalie, Kasondra, and Kearin open the large wooden wardrobe that Bridget uses for her closet. She can't believe her eyes. "Where did all of this come from?" She flops down on her bed in shock. Regan and Ana fly over to the closet, and with the help of several others, they begin to bring her the treasures. First is a shawl made of the finest Irish lace; she has seen a picture of this kind of handmade lace in the historical society achieves housed near the Book of Kells, but she didn't believe any still existed.

The parade continues with, beige leather heels, which feel like smooth butter, silk nylons, and long gloves that button at her wrist and go to her elbow, a beautiful silk slip, strapless bra, and underwear, so delicate to be almost invisible.

Then they present a gorgeous evening gown. The strapless top is a deep burgundy maroon embedded in a hundred places with Pink Austrian Crystals. The skirt is a heavenly mixture of colors ranging from a light pink to a deep burgundy and everything in between.

"This is incredible. It's not mine. Whose is it?"

"It is a gift, My Lady."

"From who? Is it ....?"

Bridget stops speaking and gawks as she spots Lord Howth; he has materialized next to her on the bed.

"I so enjoy seeing the happiness in your eyes at such little gifts." He hands her a black velvet jewelry box.

"For me?" She stares at the box. *Oh, how I wish it was a ring, or do I?*

"Please open it."

Her hands shake as she unfastens the latch. The feel of the velvet box with the deep silver etchings feels delicate; it takes her awhile. She opens what looks like a box of faeire magic. There's a rainbow of color coming from one beautiful stone on a sterling silver chain. The stone is the size of a fifty cent piece and is held in place by an intricately designed silver surround. She leans over to get next to the light and looks closer at the design. She sees a ring of faeire etched in silver. Cut so perfectly; she can tell who modeled for the piece. Her new English friends are all there; Quetip aka RaeAnne, Regan, Natalie, Cade, David, Ana, Kasondra, Alan, Deirdre, and the others who so bravely helped her succeed in this challenge.

"This is beautiful; now I have one with my English friends. You are so considerate, you know just what I would love." She looks at Mick and finds herself leaning towards him. She blushes and looks back down at the necklace. "What kind of stone is this?"

"It is a labradorite stone. So called for it was first discovered in Labrador."

"It is a way of saying that you are loved...by all." Mick says quietly.

Bridget can't help it, she cries. "Thank you so very much, I love it, it's beautiful."

Bridget hugs him and cries so hard that she starts hiccupping. The more she hiccups, the more the faeire laugh. Soon they have her laughing and dancing around the room with them. After a few minutes, she again flops down on the bed. She suppresses a yawn.

"We will leave you now to rest. Is it okay to come back later? We would love to watch you practice your curtsey," giggles Lyndsey.

Bridget laughs with them, kicks off her shoes and lays down on the bed. As she closes her eyes, she feels movement. She opens her eyes and watches her best friend, Lord Howth, now in dog form as he uses his teeth to cover her with a light throw. She sits up and pats the bed, asking Mick to join her. He jumps up on the bed and looks at her.

"Why did you turn back to dog form?"

"I believe you find it easier to speak with Mick." He muzzles her hand, and she rubs his head.

After a minute she quietly admits, "Mick, I was so worried; I thought you wouldn't come back. I thought that you were mad at me for not listening to you. I'm so sorry; I had to stop him. I couldn't let him blow up the Queen."

"I know my girl; I was angry but not with you but myself. I was not there to prevent you from getting hurt."

"I guess this is the way I am destined to learn my lessons." Bridget tries to smile as she hugs Mick.

Later Bridget joins Peter and Michelle and tries not to be a downer.

After a great takeaway Indian dinner, she and Michelle practice curtseying in front of the floor length mirror that the guys moved into the front parlor. She has never laughed so hard in her life. Whenever she stops laughing all she has to do is to look at the faeire gathered, or see the two straight-laced English gentlemen try to contain their laughter, and she bursts out laughing again.

Bridget finds that the curtsey is a difficult maneuver to execute; if it goes right it looks excellent as you descend towards the ground while shaking hands with the Queen, but if it goes wrong she can end up falling over and making a fool of herself and ruining this event for everyone. Peter told her that she could just nod her head, but she respects the Queen. If a little thing like a curtsey is a way to show that respect, then she will do it, or die trying.

Chapter 26

Marcello Tower
Howth, Ireland

Mick watches the dark clouds as they gather over the sea. The darkness of the sky well matches his mood. The sky and sea are gathering strength to hit the small tower ledge where he is sitting. Rain soaks his clothing; the wind slashes his hair against his face.

Padraig materializes next to Mick. "We watched what was happening. Bridget did it again. Our girl used her ability to close the wound and begin the healing process. She is growing stronger in her abilities and belief in herself as a warrior."

"That she is. She is accepting her gifts and is comfortable in the world of fae. My concern is that she does not yet believe that she is an equal to other humans."

Padraig sputters, his normally pale skin red with anger. "How could that be, she is more skilled than many others. There is only a handful that can close a wound. She can use the power of deduction and true faith to follow the signs given to her. Not equal..."

"We should have come into her life earlier. The challenges of her birth have left their scars. It will take time for her to overcome them. She is a special woman, but she does not yet know that."

"Will humans honor her good works?"

"Her cousin will be honored at the palace by the Queen for his part in saving the dogs, and the cathedral."

"You sound angry that she is not being recognized by humans, as one that is special. The Queen will recognize that she is special, I'm sure of it."

"She is very special," Mick says as he throws a rock far out into the Irish Sea. "The Queen and others may acknowledge the fact but until she recognizes the magic within her..."

Padraig looks at Mick for several seconds. "You are in love with her?"

"I am. Nothing I can do about it, is there?"

"Not at present, please be patient. Do you know what her feelings are?"

"She has said she loves me."

"Then that is great news!"

Mick turns to his friend, and with pain reflected in his eyes, defies his friend to laugh.

"She fell in love with a dog. She told a dog she loved him. How can she love a man who is a century older than herself and who will never grow old with her."

Chapter 27

Buckingham Palace
London, England

Bridget looks around her as the gates of Buckingham Palace opens for the limousine that Peter had hired. *This is so surreal. I know those guards are going to tell me I don't belong here.*

The driver takes them to the main entrance and Bridget lets out her breath. Charlie exits and then reaches into the limo to assist Bridget. With one hand holding the skirt of her gown in place, she swings her legs out of the car and stands. She holds onto his hand for dear life. She knows he senses her nervousness for he puts his arm through hers and with his support she somehow manages to walk past the Royal Guards and into the grand hallway.

She thought that the State Room where they were schooled in what to expect was overwhelming. It is nothing compared to the entranceway. Two sconces are holding several lights shaped like candles. They help to highlight the gold balustrade. The transition from the comparative darkness of the Grand Hall to the brightness of the Grand Staircase is amazing. She has to tell her feet to keep moving and not just stand there and gawk.

Peter is continuing his role of guide, acting as if he is not nervous. "The stairs are lit by a shallow dome of etched glass. Queen Victoria requested that the series of portraits of her immediate family be displayed around the upper part of the stairs. These include her grandparents and her parents. Thus, the portraits serve as a kind of 'receiving line' so that whoever climbs the staircase is simultaneously received by her family."

She couldn't open her eyes wide enough, not when there is so much to see. Even walking on the thick red carpet feels like she is floating. The red and gold theme is everywhere. The picture frames, candle holders, and dishes that hang on the walls are all gold. Charlie explains that they would be too heavy if they were real gold, just gold gilt covering sterling silver.

She hopes her mouth isn't hanging open when she sees the two gold thrones with red velvet cushions. Sitting upon one is a silver-haired lady with the most beautiful, warm, welcoming smile.

The Investiture in the Ballroom went by in a blur. The Queen leaves the ballroom, and they are left standing with a dozen or so members of her 'inner circle'.

Within a few minutes, the ballroom begins to fill up with various family members. Peter is like a little kid in a candy store. He and Charlie tell them who's who. Bridget sees one guy who looks to be part of a large party of people who just arrived. He looks somewhat familiar. *Why is it impossible not to think of Mick? I'm even seeing him in others now.*

Bridget nods in the direction of the door, "Charlie, who's that?"

"That gentleman belongs to the Knights of the Garter and the Royal Knights. He is speaking with Princess Alexandra, the Honorable Lady Ogilvy, The Duke of Kent, The Duke of Gloucester, The Duke of York, The Princess Royal, and The Prince of Wales..."

They hear the sound of a gentle musical note, and The Sovereign, accompanied by Prince Philip, Duke of Edinburgh, enters as if it is the Queen's first appearance in the ballroom today. Bridget is happy to see Friar Xavier walk solemnly behind the family. He looks like royalty himself until he sees her and dances up to the beautifully decorated ceiling.

"I can't believe that we are this close to the Royal Family," Bridget whispers to Michelle, who just nods. She is still speechless from having the Queen acknowledge her at Peter's investiture, and thank her for her continued care of her canine family.

"Would you care to dance?" Charlie asks. Looking so handsome in his black and white, formal tux.

Bridget smiles and takes his arm, "I would love to."

Michelle and Peter join them on the dance floor.

"Thank you for your help, Charlie, this is a dream that I don't want to end. Hope it all doesn't disappear at midnight."

"If it does, I promise to find your glass slipper and return it to you. I am a detective you know."

They laugh and twirl around the room. Charlie tells her that she is dancing the waltz. She laughs in amazement that she is even dancing, but Charlie is a good leader.

She looks around the room, suddenly feeling as though someone is watching her. *No, not just watching me, something else, some strong feeling, but not evil.*

"That guy over there by the column is staring at us. I asked you his name earlier, but you rattled off so many names I don't remember his. Why do you think he's staring?"

"That is Lord Howth. He stares at every beautiful woman. Would you like to meet him?"

How on earth did I not recognize Mick? "Wait I..."

Charlie has her by the hand, and they walk across the dance floor to meet Mick, all decked out as the Royal Lord that he is.

"Hi Michael, how are you? I thought you were still at your summer home in Scotland?" Charlie asks.

"Good Evening Charles, a little business to do in town. I will be heading back up North soon."

"May I introduce you to a good friend of mine? Bridget, this is Lord Howth."

Bridget just knows she is turning a bright red. How did she not recognize Mick? The lights are dim, but she should know him anywhere. Of course, she has never seen him dressed so elegantly.

"How do you do Lord Howth. I hope I'm not supposed to curtsey. I accomplished that once today, and hope never to have to do it again."

Mick laughs and has a twinkle in his beautiful light brown eyes. They are more like amber, shining with life, and yet his smile can't hide a tinge of sadness. She wonders what could make this gorgeous hunk of manhood sad. He says something about calling him Michael and laughs some more. All traces of sadness is gone. *Did I imagine it?*

"Charlie, may I ask your lady for a dance?" Mick asks. Charlie nods. "Of course my friend."

"I would love to dance, thank you," Bridget says.

Bridget takes Mick's arm and when they are on the dance floor says, "Okay, out with it, how do you know Charlie?"

"Simple, I checked him out when he first sent you that card telling you of his advancement."

"Checked him out how?"

"I accidently bumped into him and spilled his coffee. Of course, to make good, I invited him to my club."

She looks up at him and frowns. "Hmm."

"By the way, I approve of him." He announces.

Bridget can't help but giggle at her high and mighty lord.

Lord Howth and Bridget dance the next three dances. They talk when they can, but she can't remember what was said. She feels as though she is floating on air. She cherishes her friendship with Mick. She won't ruin it by wishing things could be different. She will be grateful for the friendship she has. Sighing loudly she says, "I really wish I could tell everyone I know you."

"Well, now that we are officially introduced you can." Mick looks down at her and smiles, but he senses a deep sadness in Bridget, he must find out what is troubling her. "Would you like to walk out on the terrace for a bit of air?"

"I'd love to." As they pass the other women in the room, no matter what their age, Bridget is shocked to see that they are all trying to get Mick's attention. Mick is like Prince Charming, and she feels like Cinderella before the ball.

She looks around at the palace garden; it is lit by a thousand tiny lights hung strategically among the trees. Bridget feels as if she's in a dream.

She is holding Mick's arm; her surroundings are perfect she really doesn't want to ruin the evening, but this is hanging on and must be done.

Well, no time like the present. I better get this over with. "Mick I won't be going back to Ireland. I have talked with Peter and decided to join him in his work at the detective agency. First, I need to find an apartment..."

Mick stops walking and looks down at Bridget. A thousand thoughts and fears are rushing around in his head. He blurts out, "Wonderful news. You may keep the flat in Battersea, as my gift to you. Although you can afford a much nicer place with your inheritance."

Bridget is shocked. She was ready for an argument. Threats of her not being ready to defend herself. Anything on his part to make her stay, to keep her by his side. Not a goodbye present. She is barely able to mumble a quiet, "Thank you."

Totally uncomfortable now, she looks back to where Charlie is sitting by himself, "I'm sorry Mick. I'm a horrible date. Charlie is all alone. Please take me back to our table."

"Of course, right away." As they walk he asks, "Are you in love with my friend Charlie?"

Bridget snaps back, "That's none of your business. We're friends, and I don't intentionally neglect my friends."

At the table, Lord Howth apologizes to Charlie.

"Sorry old chap." He pulls out a chair for Bridget. "Sorry, we took so long. I don't know what came over me. It must have been the lobster."

He turns to Bridget and winks. His eyes are like warm honey. He holds her hand.

With a slight nod of his head, he brings her hand to his lips and at the last minute, turns her wrist to the area not covered in material and kisses it. She just stands there in shock watching him. He looks into her eyes and gives her one of the saddest smiles she has ever seen.

Luckily she is standing by her chair. Otherwise, she would have fallen. She can still feel the burn from those lips on her skin.

"What was that Michael said about a lobster?" asks an amused Charlie.

"Lobster?" Bridget looks after Lord Howth as he leaves the hall.

"Remember I told you about the guy who helped me up at the reception when I was wearing a lobster on my head. That's him." Everyone laughs, except Bridget. She looks around, but Mick has left the ballroom. The rest of the night is a blur.

She gets home, so wired she knows she can't possibly sleep, but soon she's in a deep slumber.

The wind's blowing, the rain is pouring down, she has to hurry! Someone is in danger. Someone important to her life. Someone in pain.

She jumps up in a state of near panic, the dream already a blur. She uses her breath to slow down her heartbeat. She's surprised she didn't call for Mick so that she could talk about her dream.

Her subconscious knows she must get used to being on her own, but it doesn't mean she has to like it. She pats the bed beside her and thinks of what Mick would say.

"You are ready to face anything Bridget. It was foretold that you would meet Morrigan and defeat her at Barnacogue. You did that. You will be safe. There is no evil you cannot defeat."

She looks at the empty place beside her and asks, "Then why am I so scared?"

THE END?

Made in the USA
San Bernardino, CA
28 September 2016